BRETT BEAN

ZOO PATROL SQUAD

RUN, MONSTER, RUN!

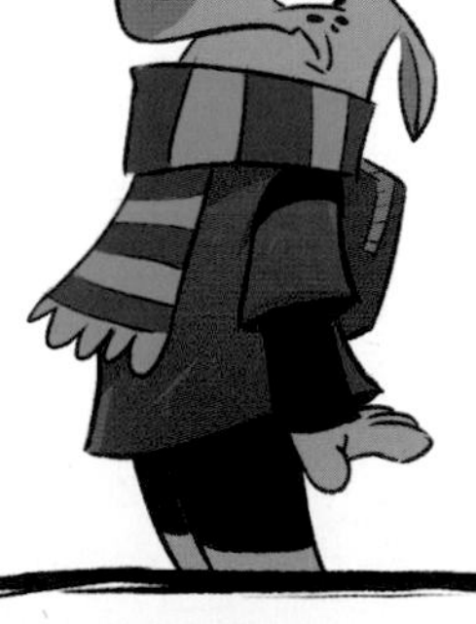

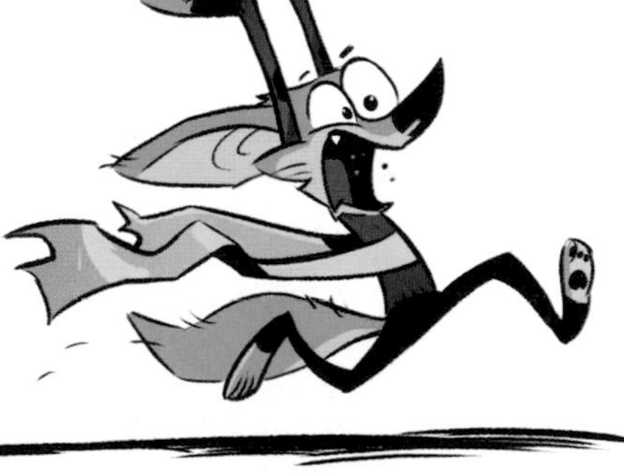

PENGUIN WORKSHOP

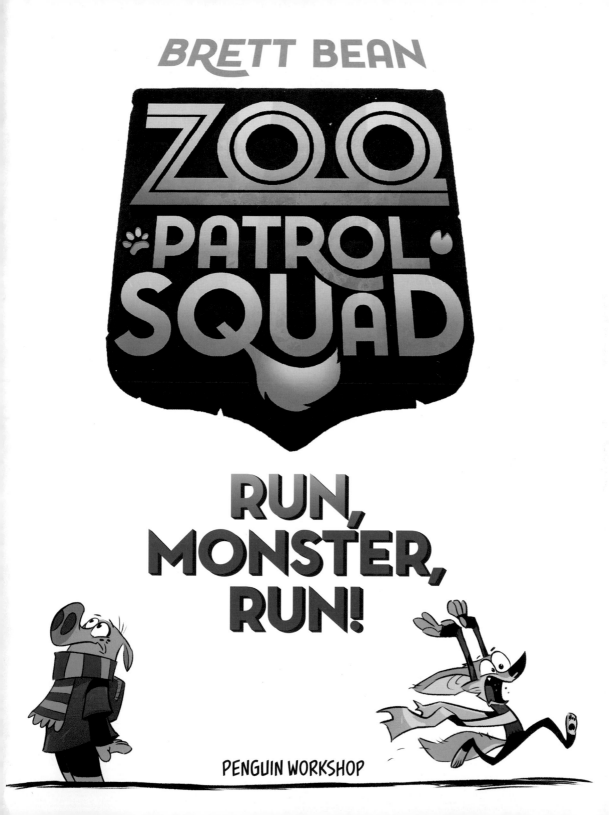

NOTE FROM THE AUTHOR

For my wife, my constant mess of inspiration.
Thank you for the time needed to make this dream come true.

For my kids. Thanks to you,
I try to make this world a better place than how I found it.

For Mom, you know.

ABOUT THE CREATOR

Brett Bean is an author, illustrator, and designer whose work has been featured across film, TV, comics, children's books, and more. He has lots of artwork and designs on his website, brettbean.com.
He works from Los Angeles.

To learn more about the Zoo Patrol Squad, go to zoopatrolsquad.com.

W

PENGUIN WORKSHOP
An Imprint of Penguin Random House LLC, New York

Visit us online at www.penguinrandomhouse.com.

Library of Congress Control Number: 2020029361

ISBN 9780593093733   10 9 8 7 6 5 4 3 2 1

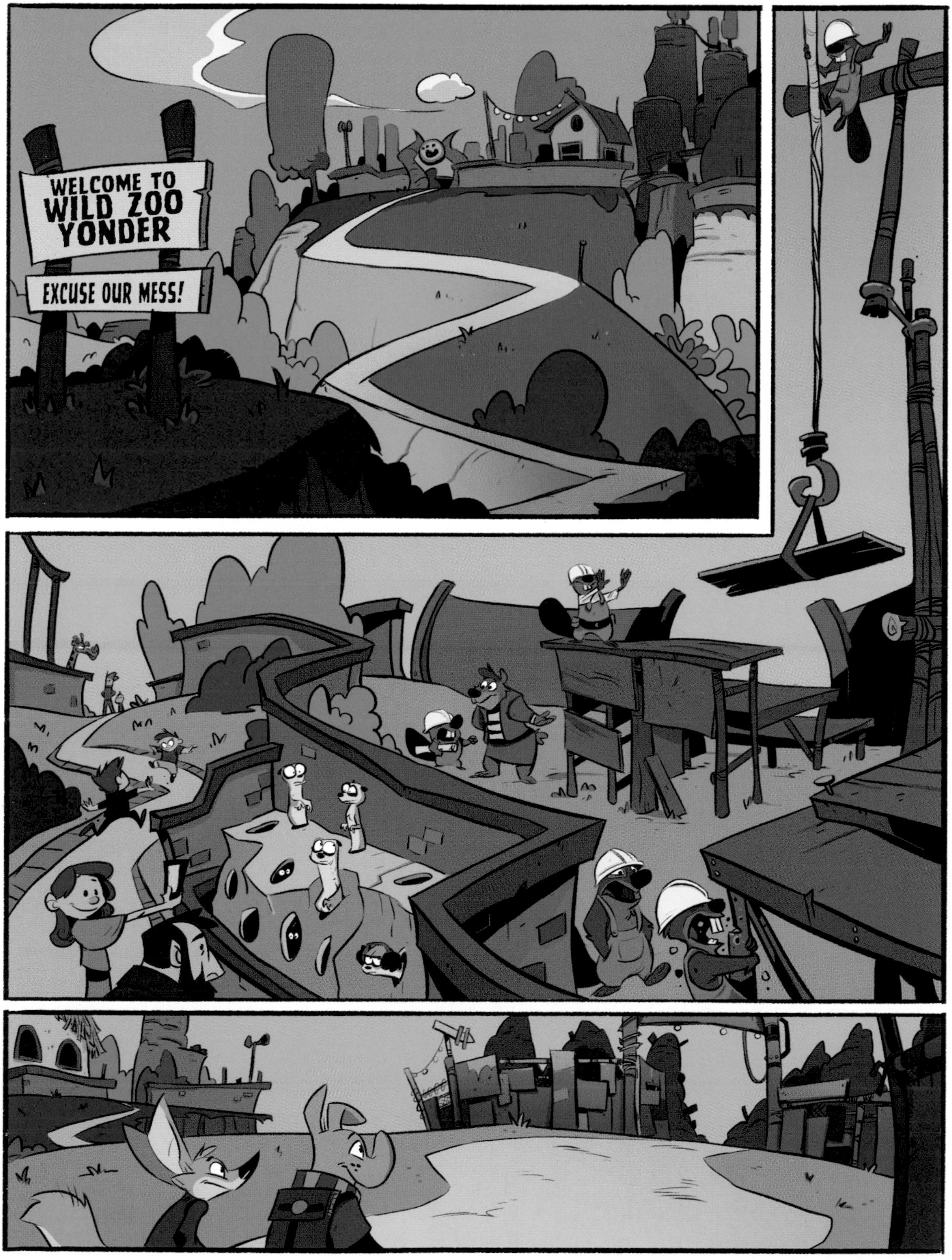
WELCOME TO WILD ZOO YONDER
EXCUSE OUR MESS!

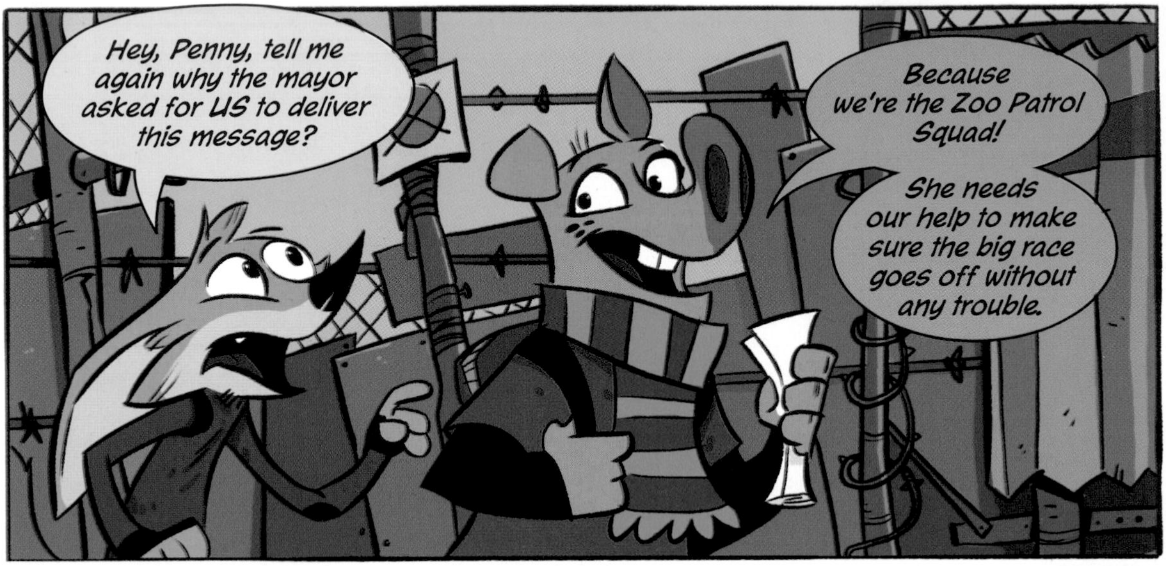
Hey, Penny, tell me again why the mayor asked for US to deliver this message?
Because we're the Zoo Patrol Squad!
She needs our help to make sure the big race goes off without any trouble.

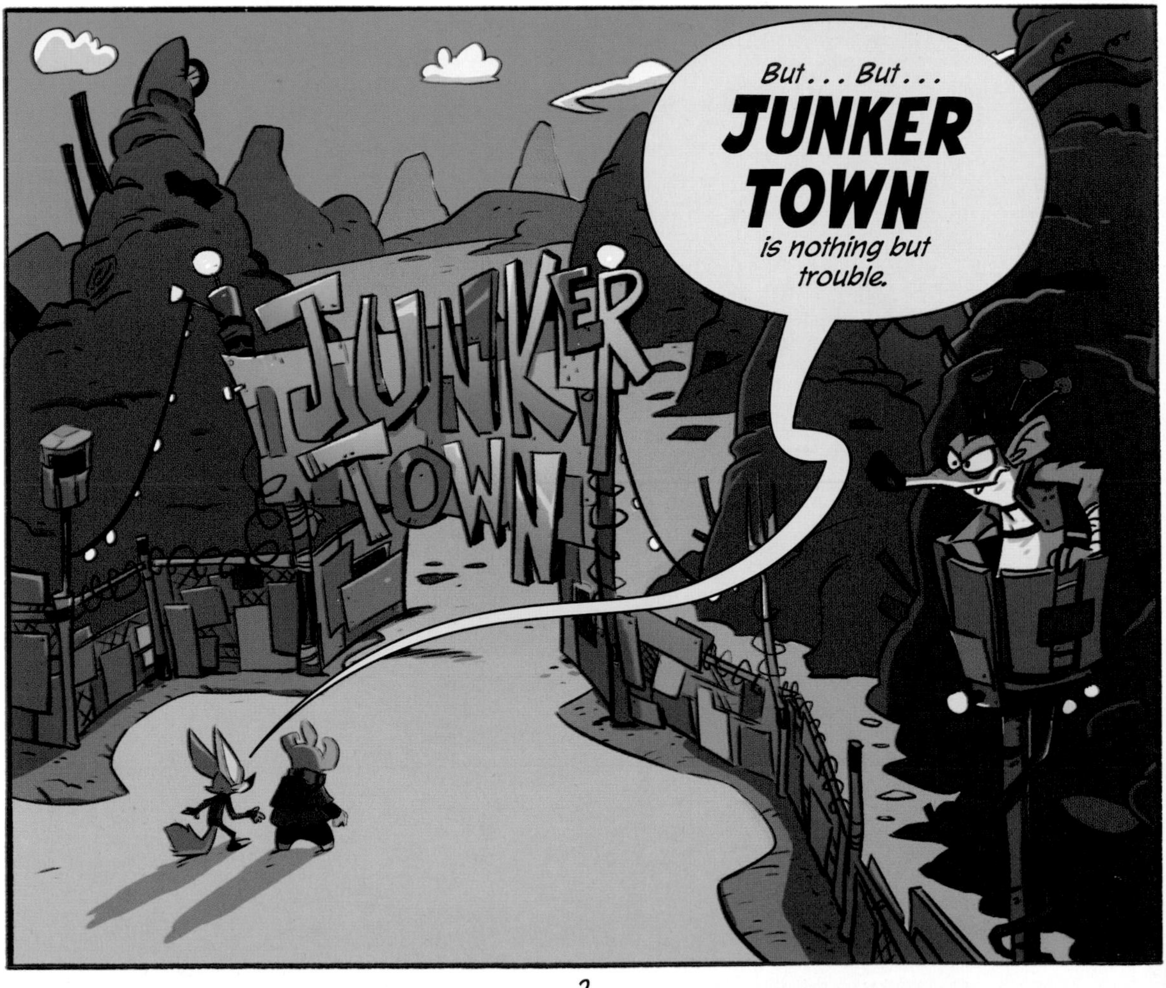
JUNKER TOWN
But... But... JUNKER TOWN is nothing but trouble.

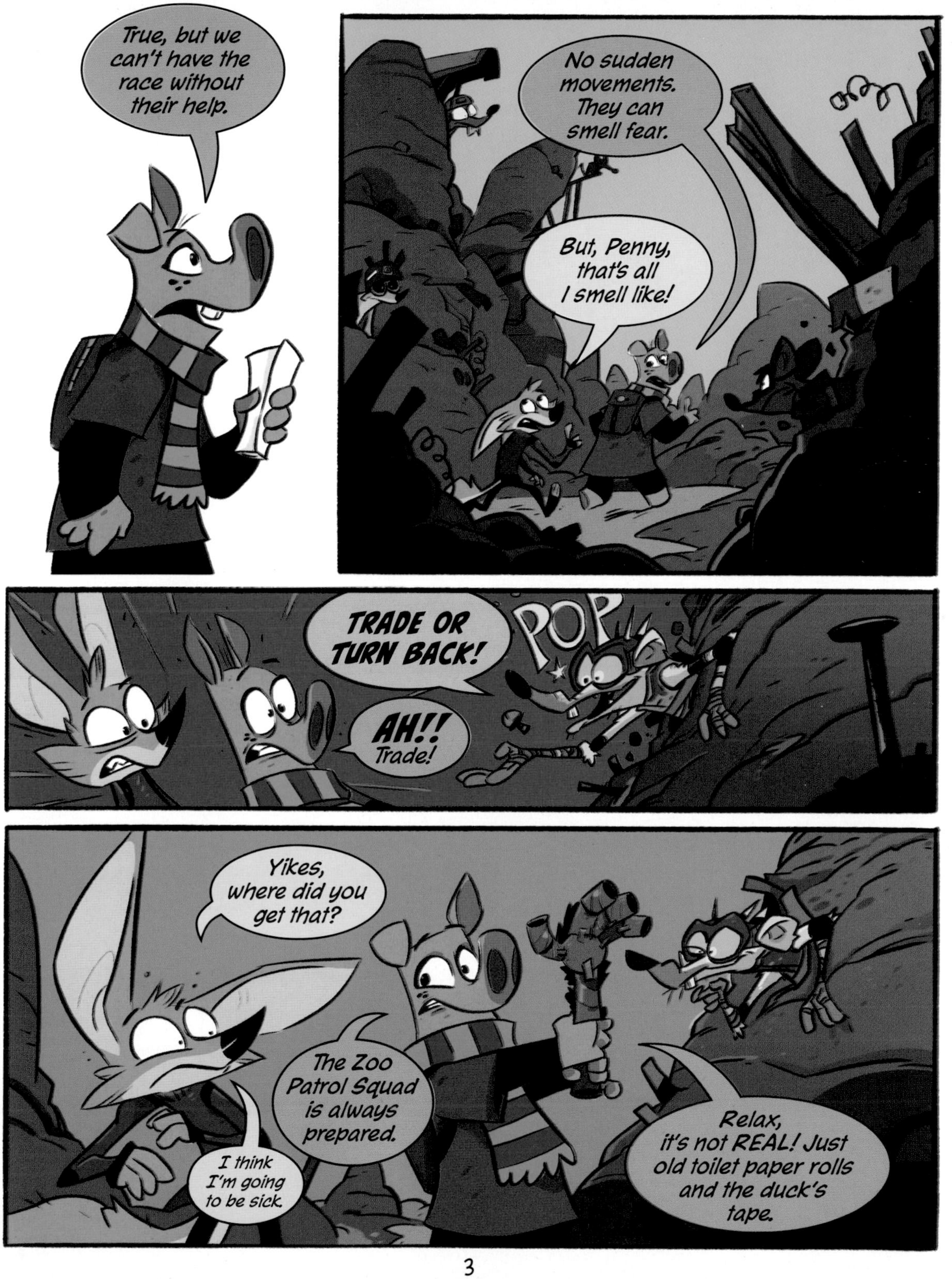

True, but we can't have the race without their help.
No sudden movements. They can smell fear.
But, Penny, that's all I smell like!
TRADE OR TURN BACK!
POP
AH!! Trade!
Yikes, where did you get that?
The Zoo Patrol Squad is always prepared.
I think I'm going to be sick.
Relax, it's not REAL! Just old toilet paper rolls and the duck's tape.

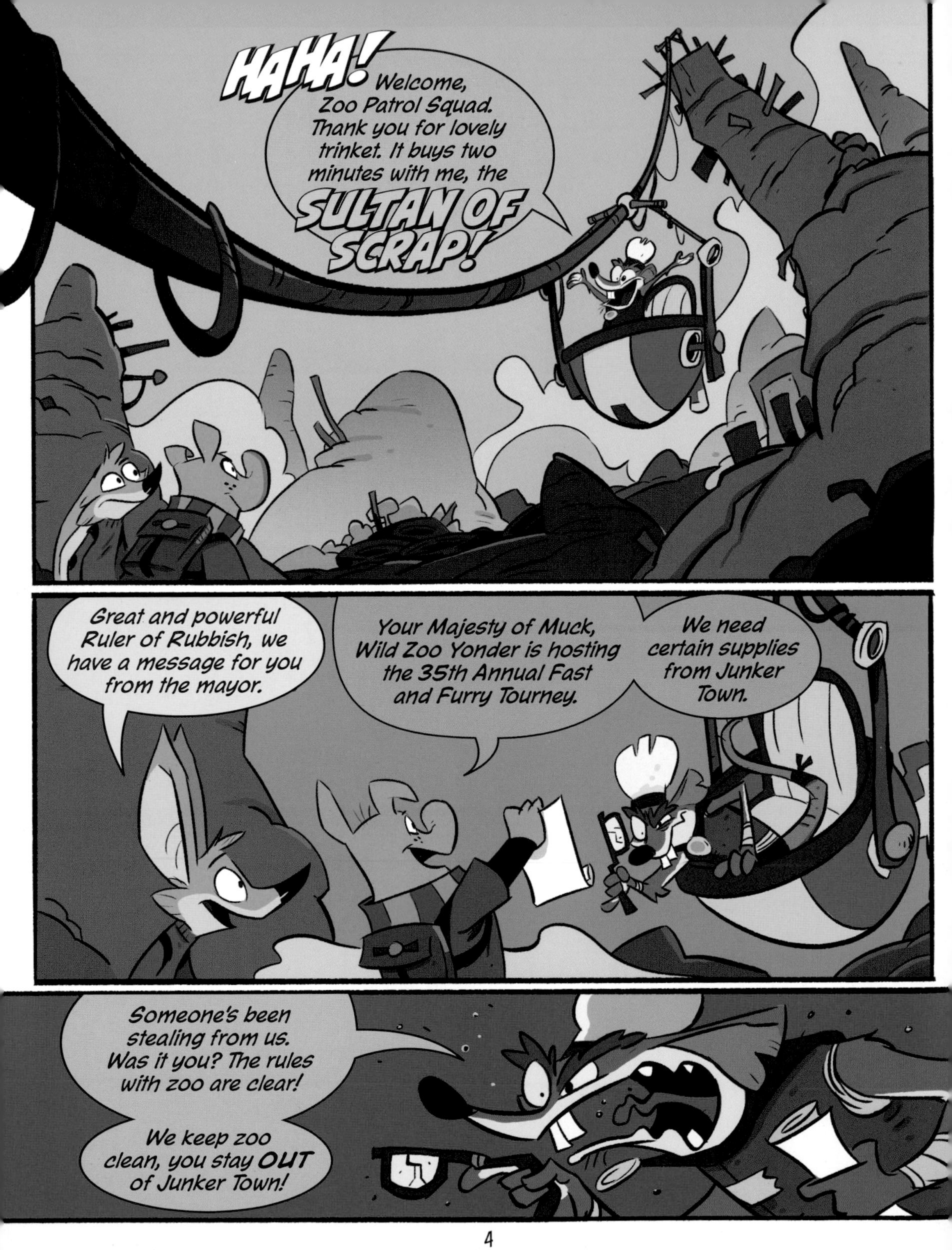
HAHA! Welcome, Zoo Patrol Squad. Thank you for lovely trinket. It buys two minutes with me, the SULTAN OF SCRAP!
Great and powerful Ruler of Rubbish, we have a message for you from the mayor.
Your Majesty of Muck, Wild Zoo Yonder is hosting the 35th Annual Fast and Furry Tourney.
We need certain supplies from Junker Town.
Someone's been stealing from us. Was it you? The rules with zoo are clear!
We keep zoo clean, you stay OUT of Junker Town!

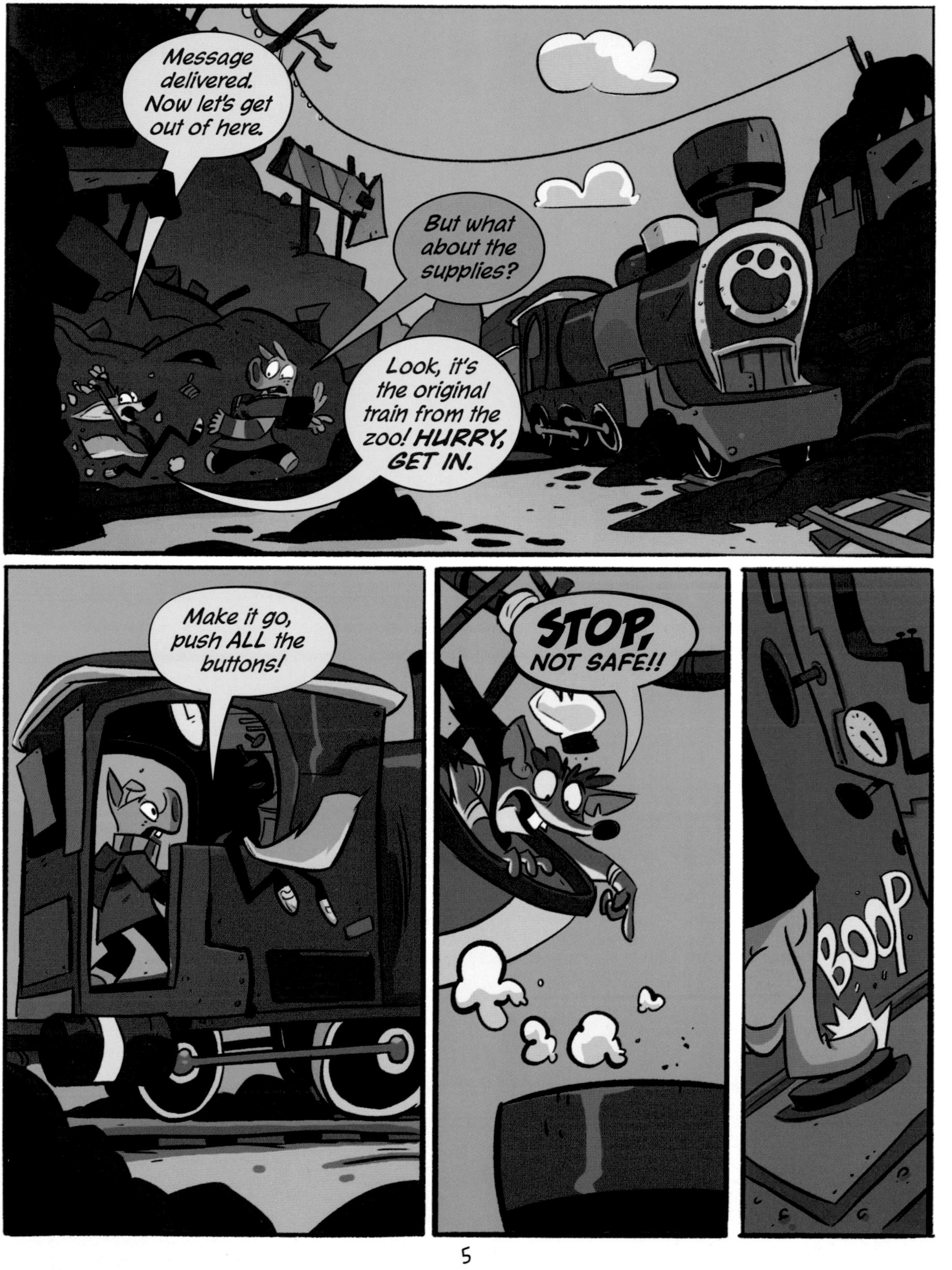
Message delivered. Now let's get out of here.
But what about the supplies?
Look, it's the original train from the zoo! HURRY, GET IN.
Make it go, push ALL the buttons!
STOP, NOT SAFE!!
BOOP

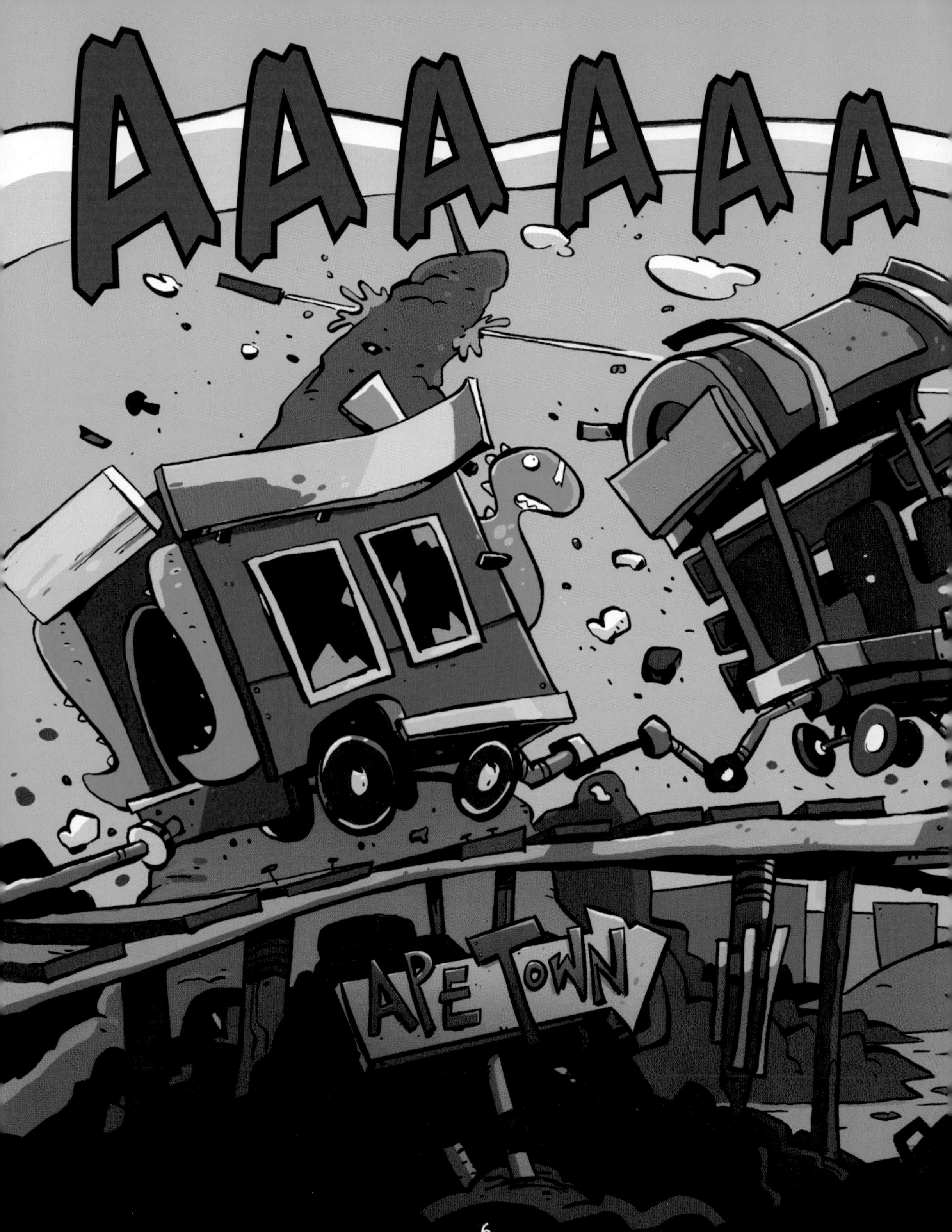
AAAAAA
APE TOWN

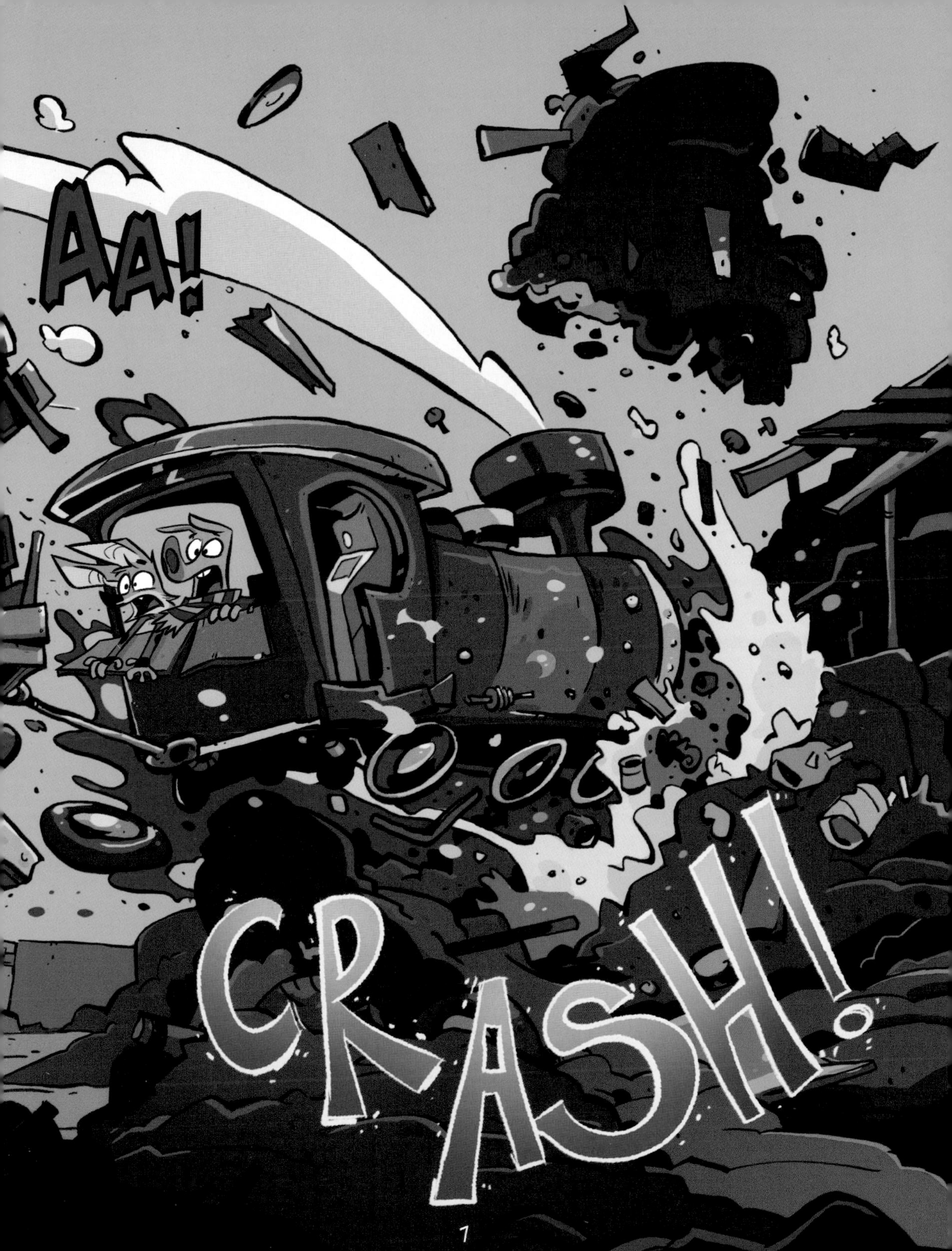
AA!
CRASH!

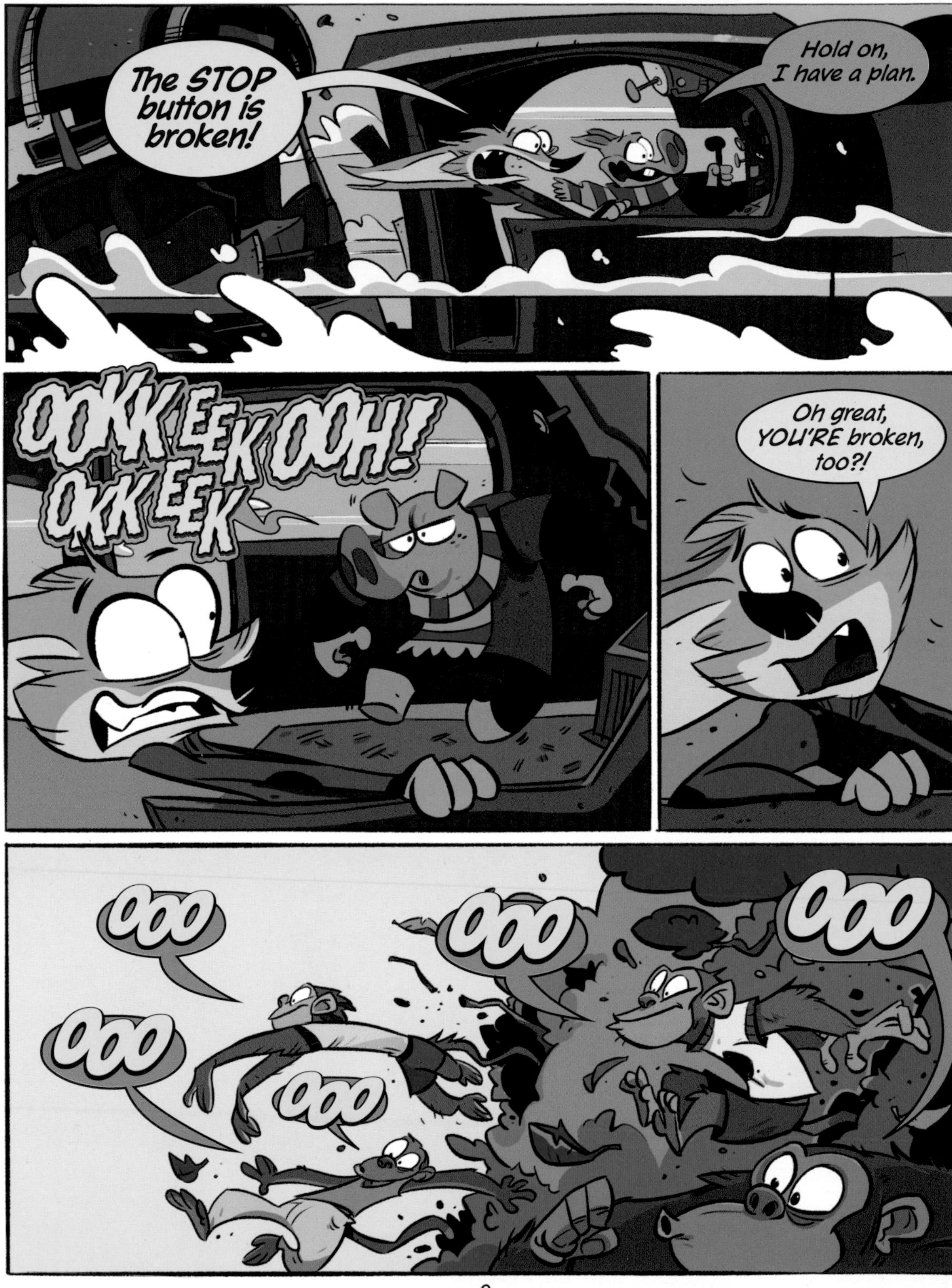
The STOP button is broken!
Hold on, I have a plan.
OOKK EEK OOH! OKK EEK
Oh great, YOU'RE broken, too?!
OOO
OOO
OOO
OOO
OOO

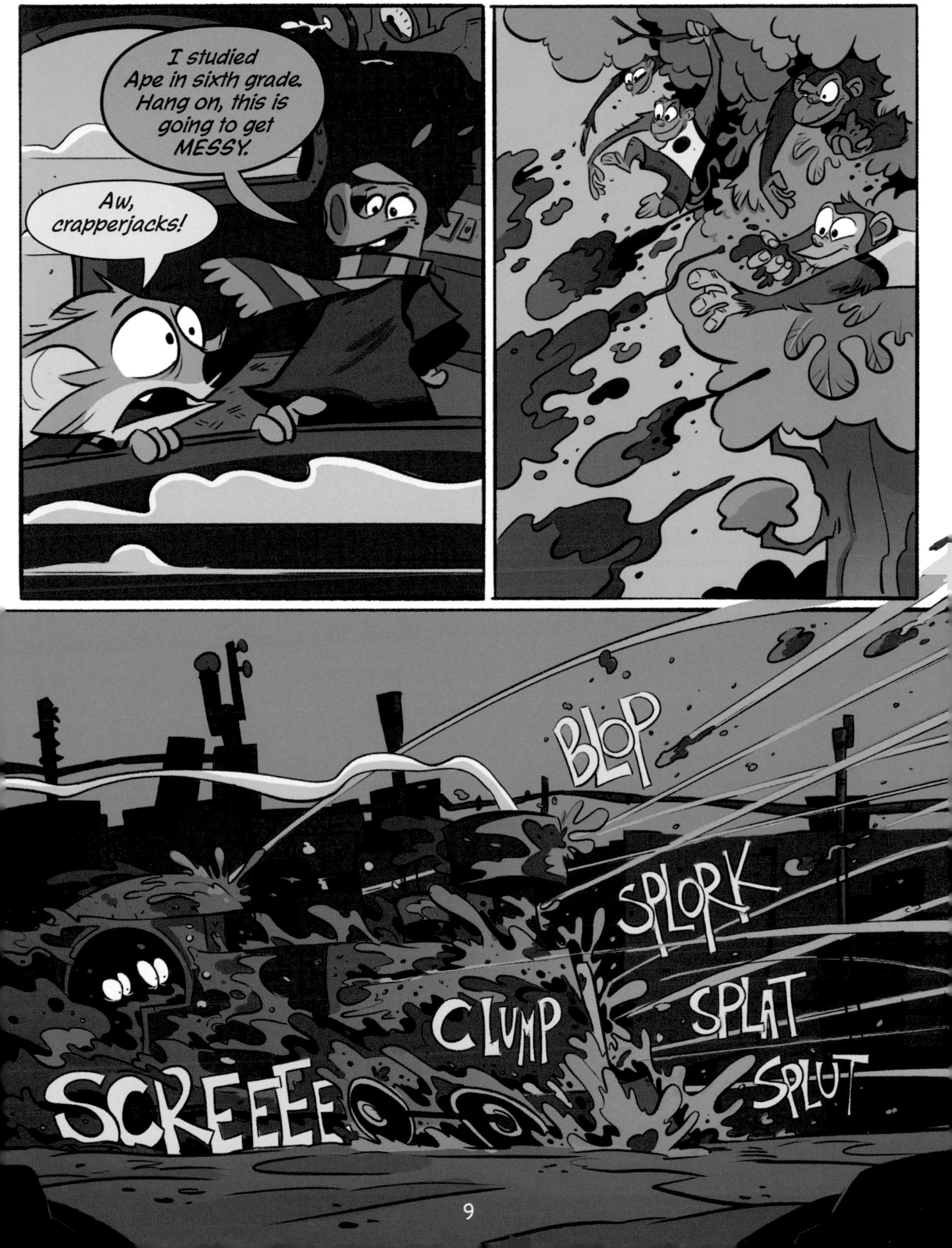

I studied Ape in sixth grade. Hang on, this is going to get MESSY.
Aw, crapperjacks!
BLOP
SPLORK
SPLAT
CLUMP
SPLUT
SCREEEEE

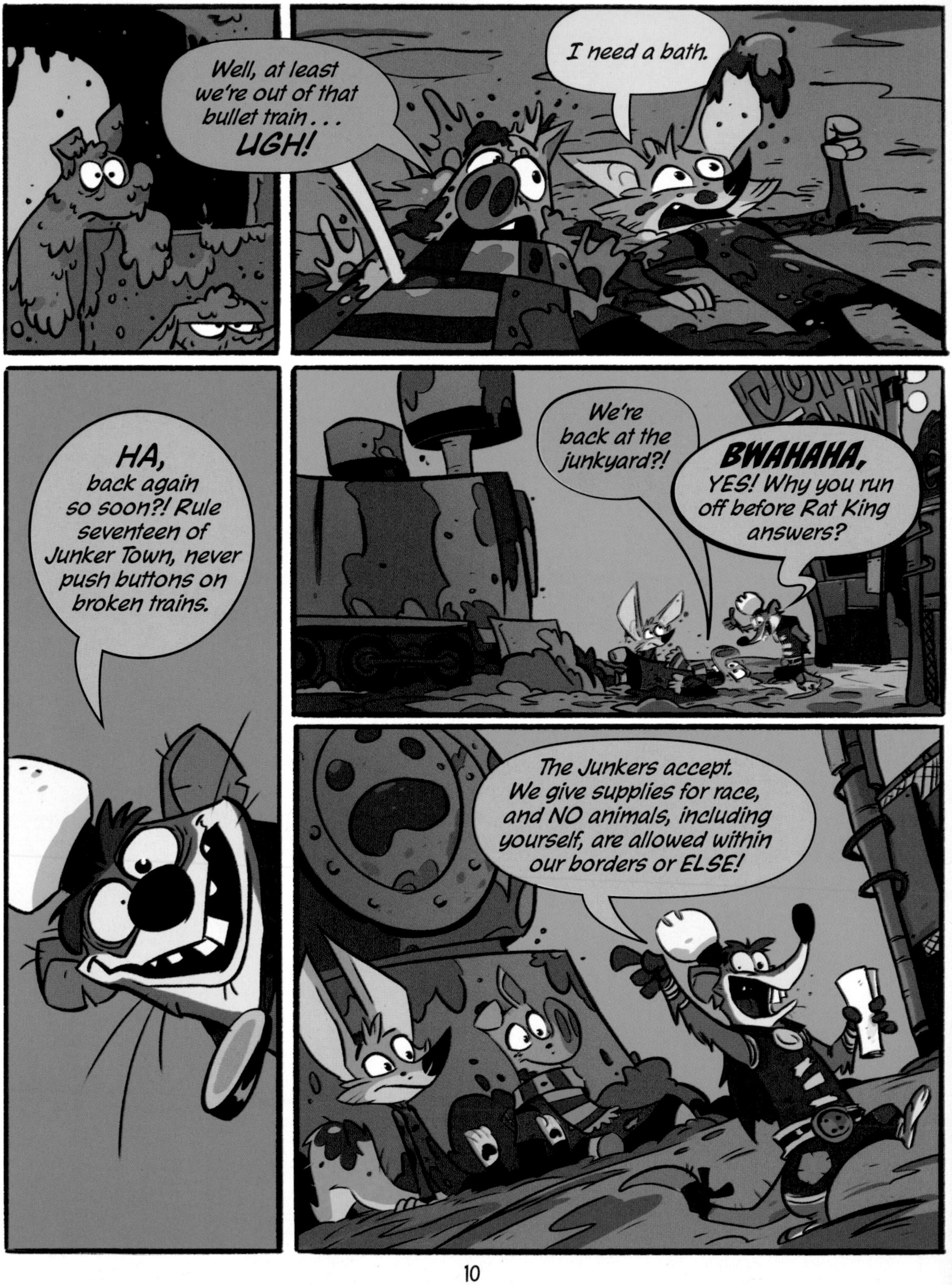
Well, at least we're out of that bullet train . . . UGH!
I need a bath.
HA, back again so soon?! Rule seventeen of Junker Town, never push buttons on broken trains.
We're back at the junkyard?!
BWAHAHA, YES! Why you run off before Rat King answers?
The Junkers accept. We give supplies for race, and NO animals, including yourself, are allowed within our borders or ELSE!

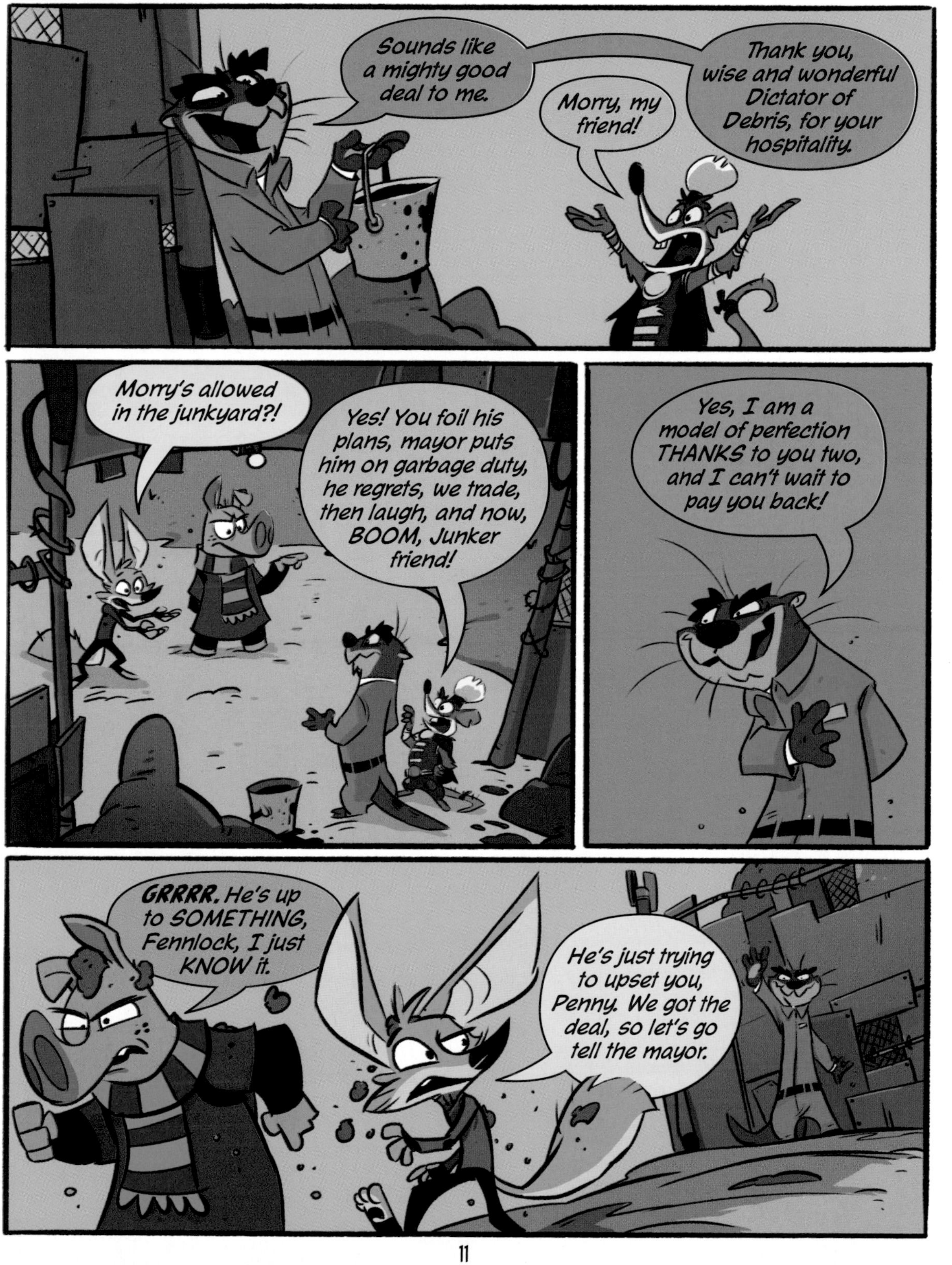
Sounds like a mighty good deal to me.
Morry, my friend!
Thank you, wise and wonderful Dictator of Debris, for your hospitality.
Morry's allowed in the junkyard?!
Yes! You foil his plans, mayor puts him on garbage duty, he regrets, we trade, then laugh, and now, BOOM, Junker friend!
Yes, I am a model of perfection THANKS to you two, and I can't wait to pay you back!
GRRRR. He's up to SOMETHING, Fennlock, I just KNOW it.
He's just trying to upset you, Penny. We got the deal, so let's go tell the mayor.

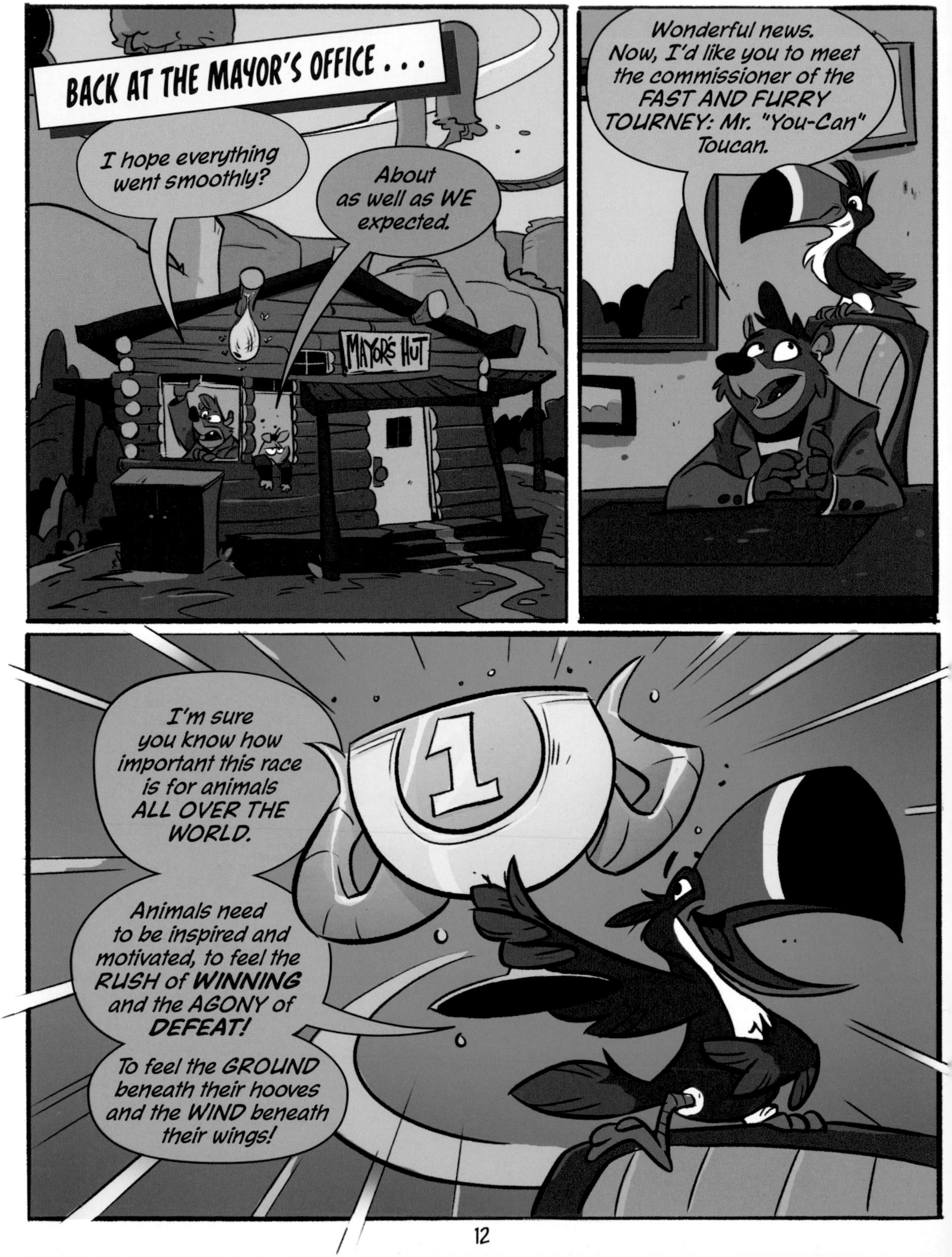
BACK AT THE MAYOR'S OFFICE . . .
I hope everything went smoothly?
About as well as WE expected.
MAYOR'S HUT
Wonderful news. Now, I'd like you to meet the commissioner of the FAST AND FURRY TOURNEY: Mr. "You-Can" Toucan.
I'm sure you know how important this race is for animals ALL OVER THE WORLD.
Animals need to be inspired and motivated, to feel the RUSH of WINNING and the AGONY of DEFEAT!
To feel the GROUND beneath their hooves and the WIND beneath their wings!

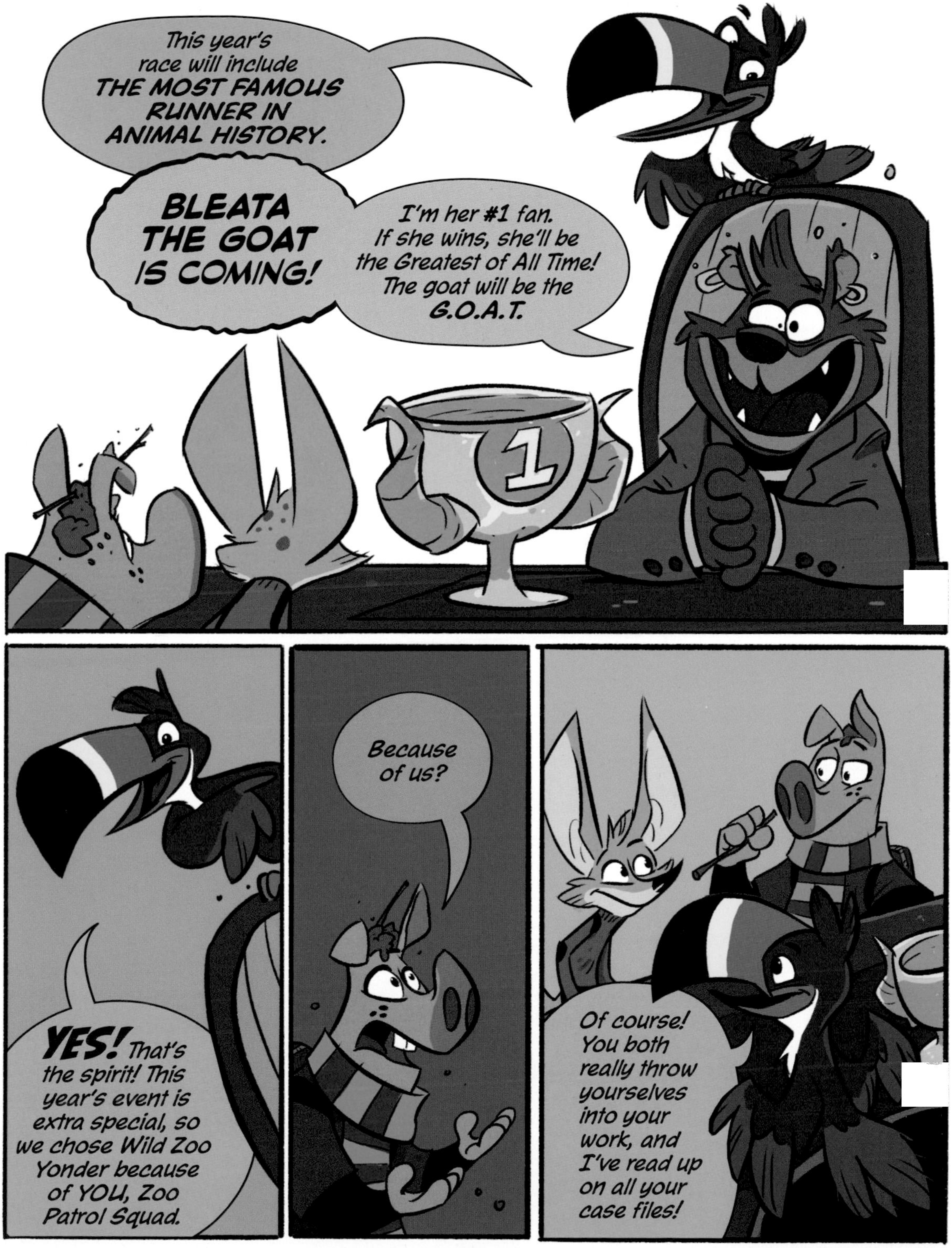
This year's race will include THE MOST FAMOUS RUNNER IN ANIMAL HISTORY.
BLEATA THE GOAT IS COMING!
I'm her #1 fan. If she wins, she'll be the Greatest of All Time! The goat will be the G.O.A.T.
YES! That's the spirit! This year's event is extra special, so we chose Wild Zoo Yonder because of YOU, Zoo Patrol Squad.
Because of us?
Of course! You both really throw yourselves into your work, and I've read up on all your case files!

CASE NO. TWENTY-SIX

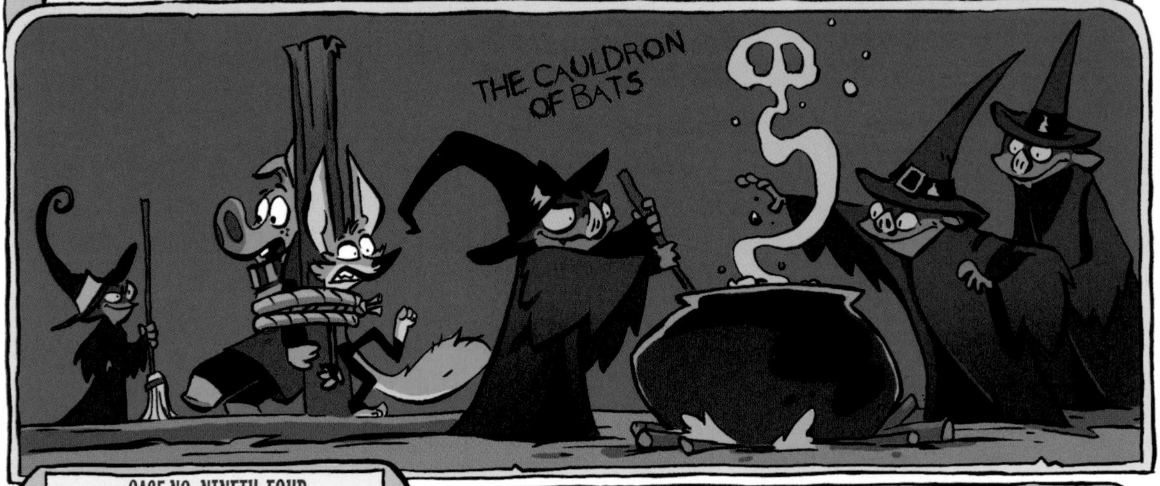
THE CAULDRON OF BATS

CASE NO. NINETY-FOUR

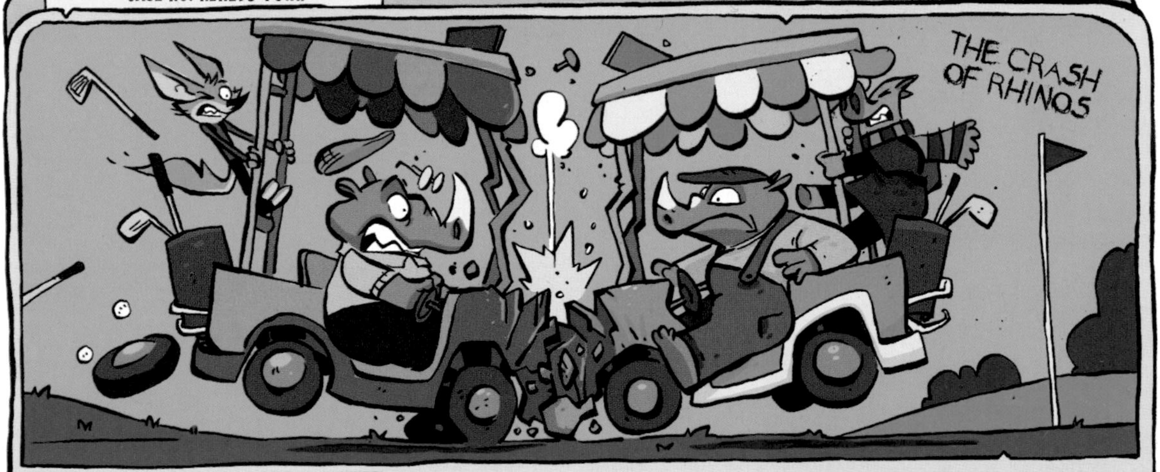
THE CRASH OF RHINOS

CASE NO. FOUR

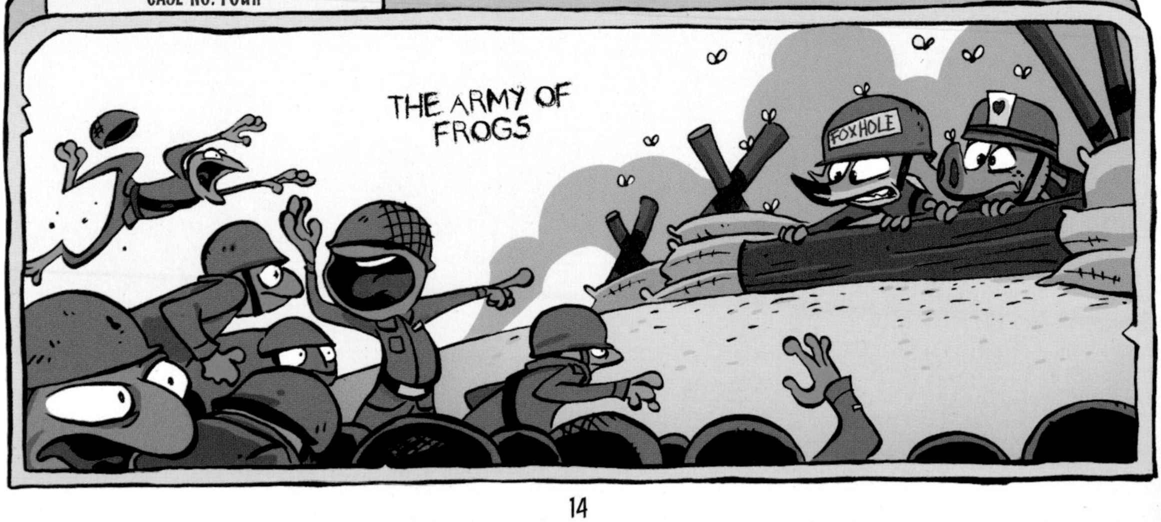
THE ARMY OF FROGS
FOXHOLE

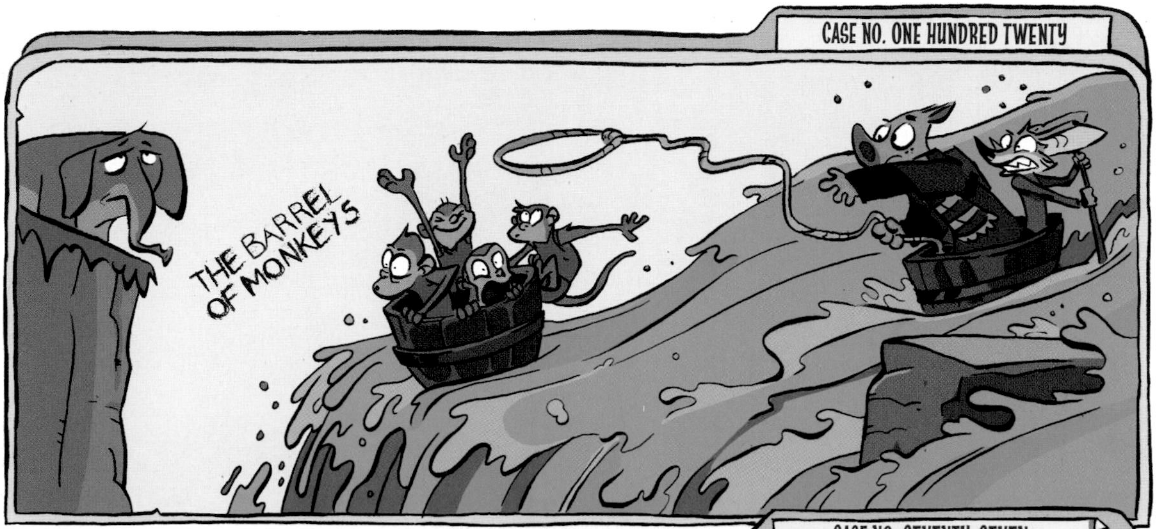
CASE NO. ONE HUNDRED TWENTY
THE BARREL OF MONKEYS

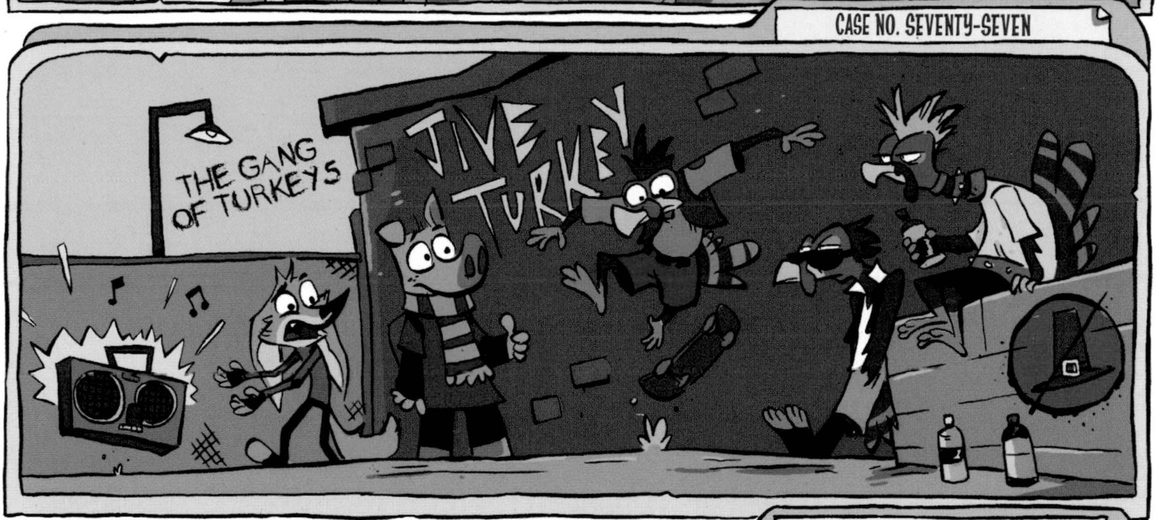
CASE NO. SEVENTY-SEVEN
THE GANG OF TURKEYS
JIVE TURKEY

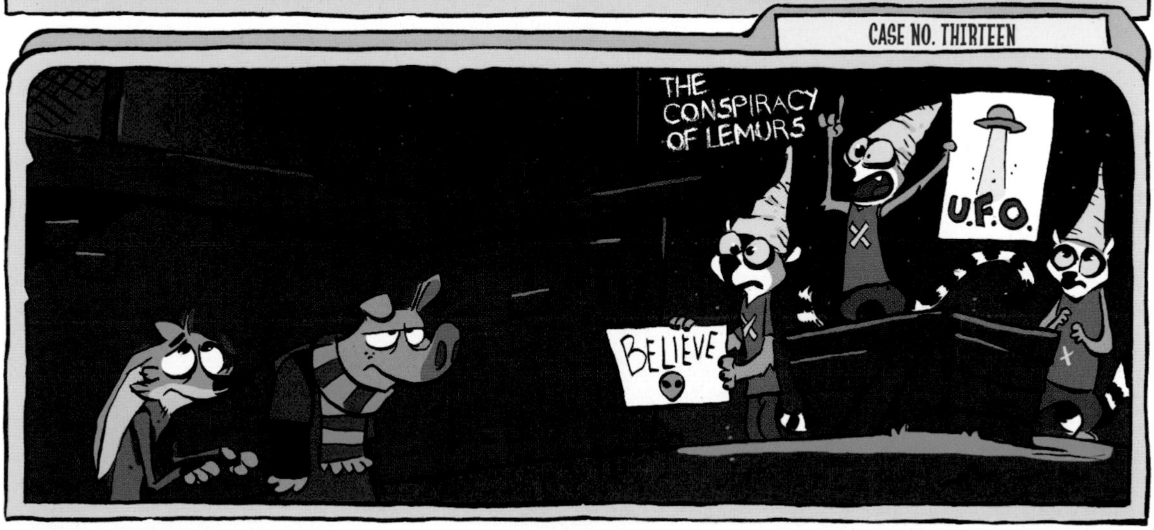
CASE NO. THIRTEEN
THE CONSPIRACY OF LEMURS
U.F.O.
BELIEVE

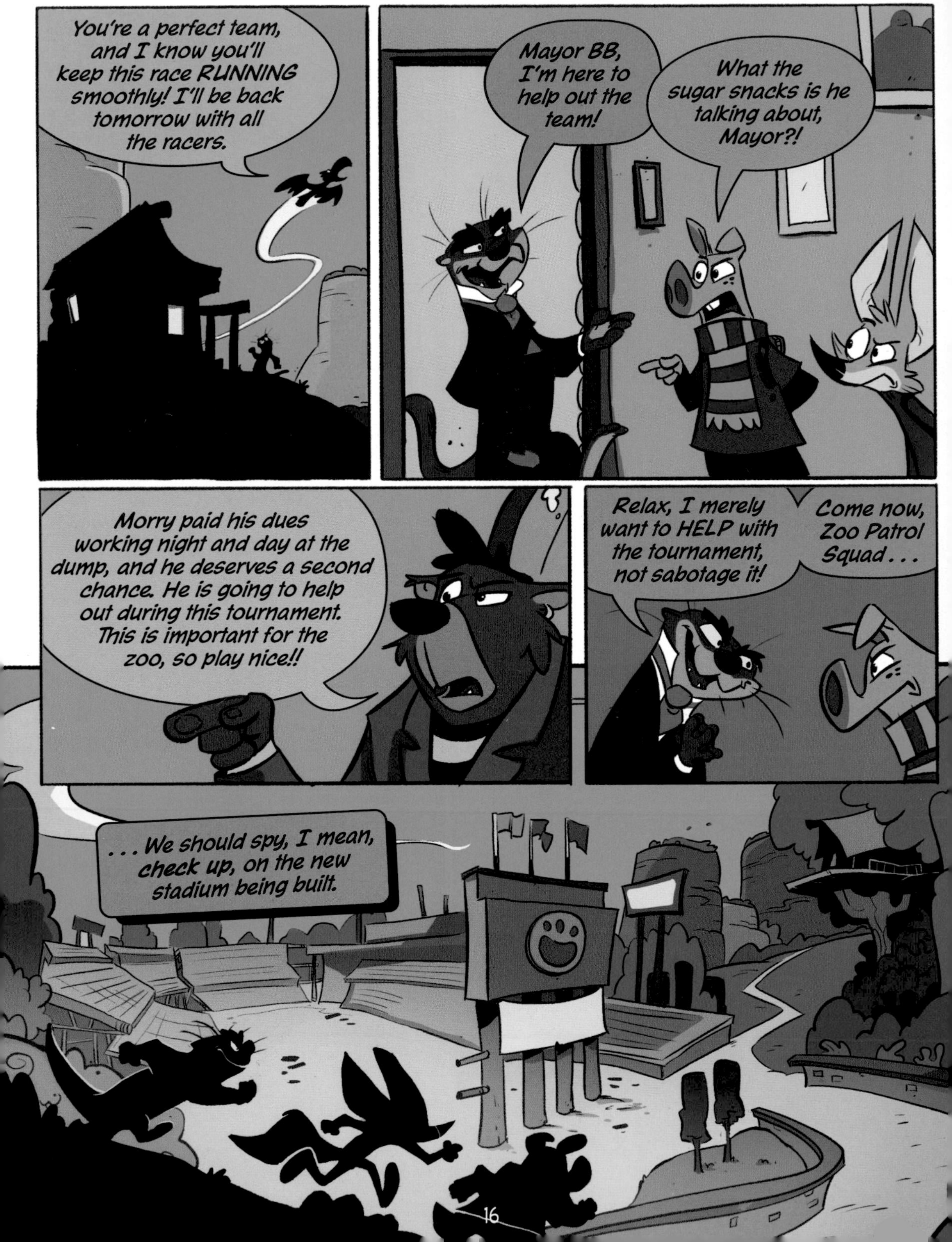

You're a perfect team, and I know you'll keep this race RUNNING smoothly! I'll be back tomorrow with all the racers.
Mayor BB, I'm here to help out the team!
What the sugar snacks is he talking about, Mayor?!
Morry paid his dues working night and day at the dump, and he deserves a second chance. He is going to help out during this tournament. This is important for the zoo, so play nice!!
Relax, I merely want to HELP with the tournament, not sabotage it!
Come now, Zoo Patrol Squad . . .
. . . We should spy, I mean, check up, on the new stadium being built.

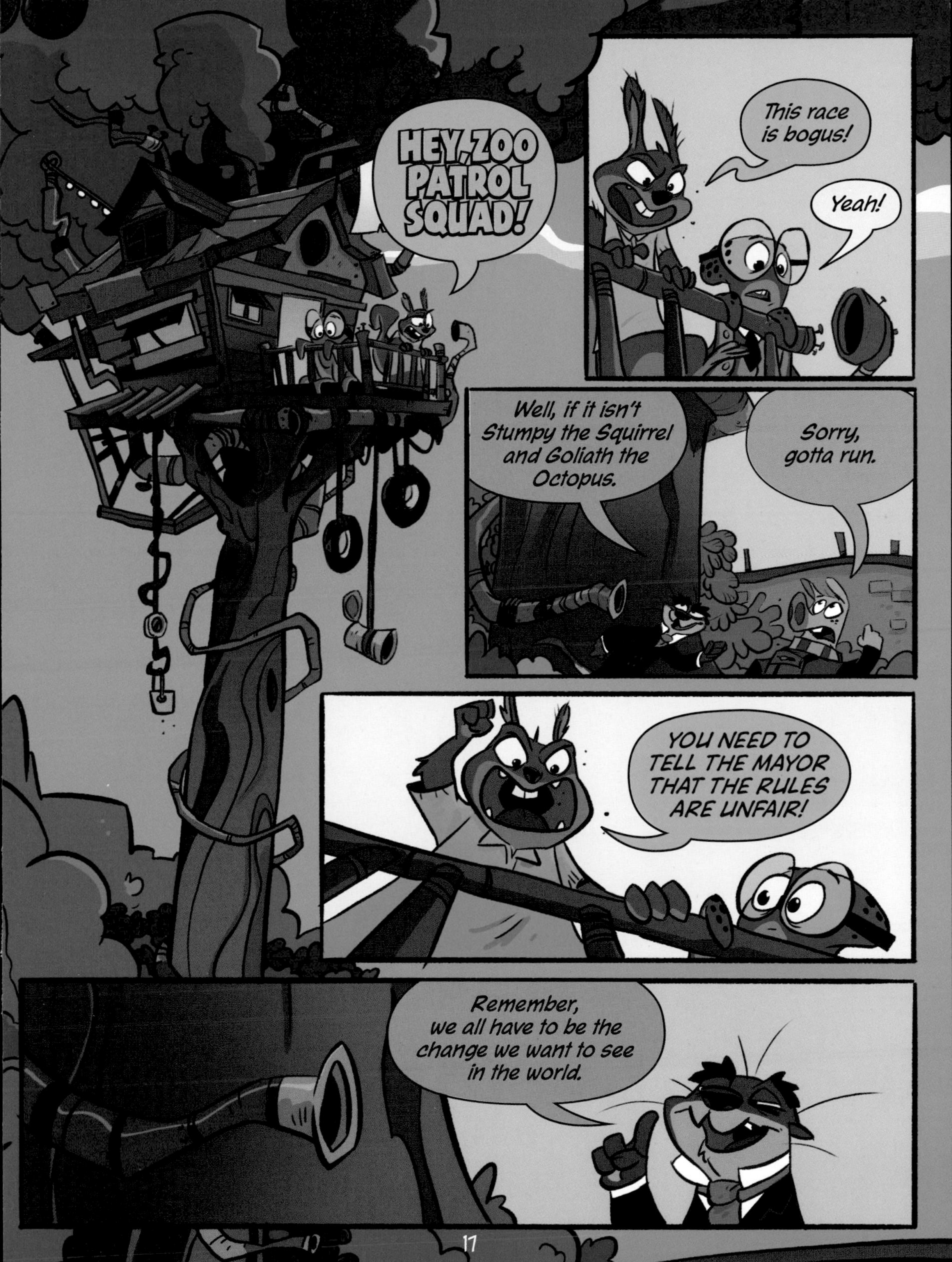
HEY, ZOO PATROL SQUAD!
This race is bogus!
Yeah!
Well, if it isn't Stumpy the Squirrel and Goliath the Octopus.
Sorry, gotta run.
YOU NEED TO TELL THE MAYOR THAT THE RULES ARE UNFAIR!
Remember, we all have to be the change we want to see in the world.

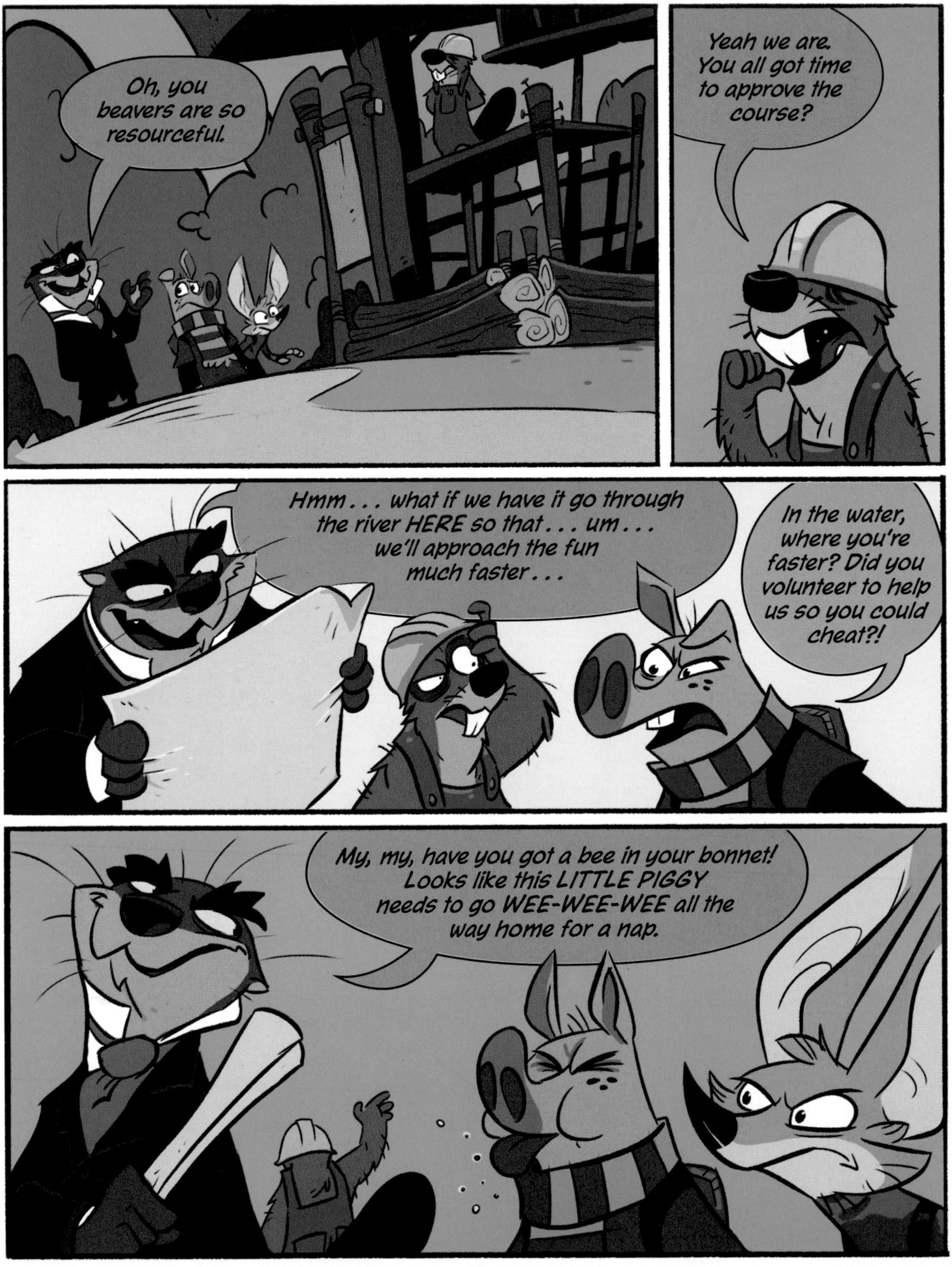
Oh, you beavers are so resourceful.
Yeah we are. You all got time to approve the course?
Hmm . . . what if we have it go through the river HERE so that . . . um . . . we'll approach the fun much faster . . .
In the water, where you're faster? Did you volunteer to help us so you could cheat?!
My, my, have you got a bee in your bonnet! Looks like this LITTLE PIGGY needs to go WEE-WEE-WEE all the way home for a nap.

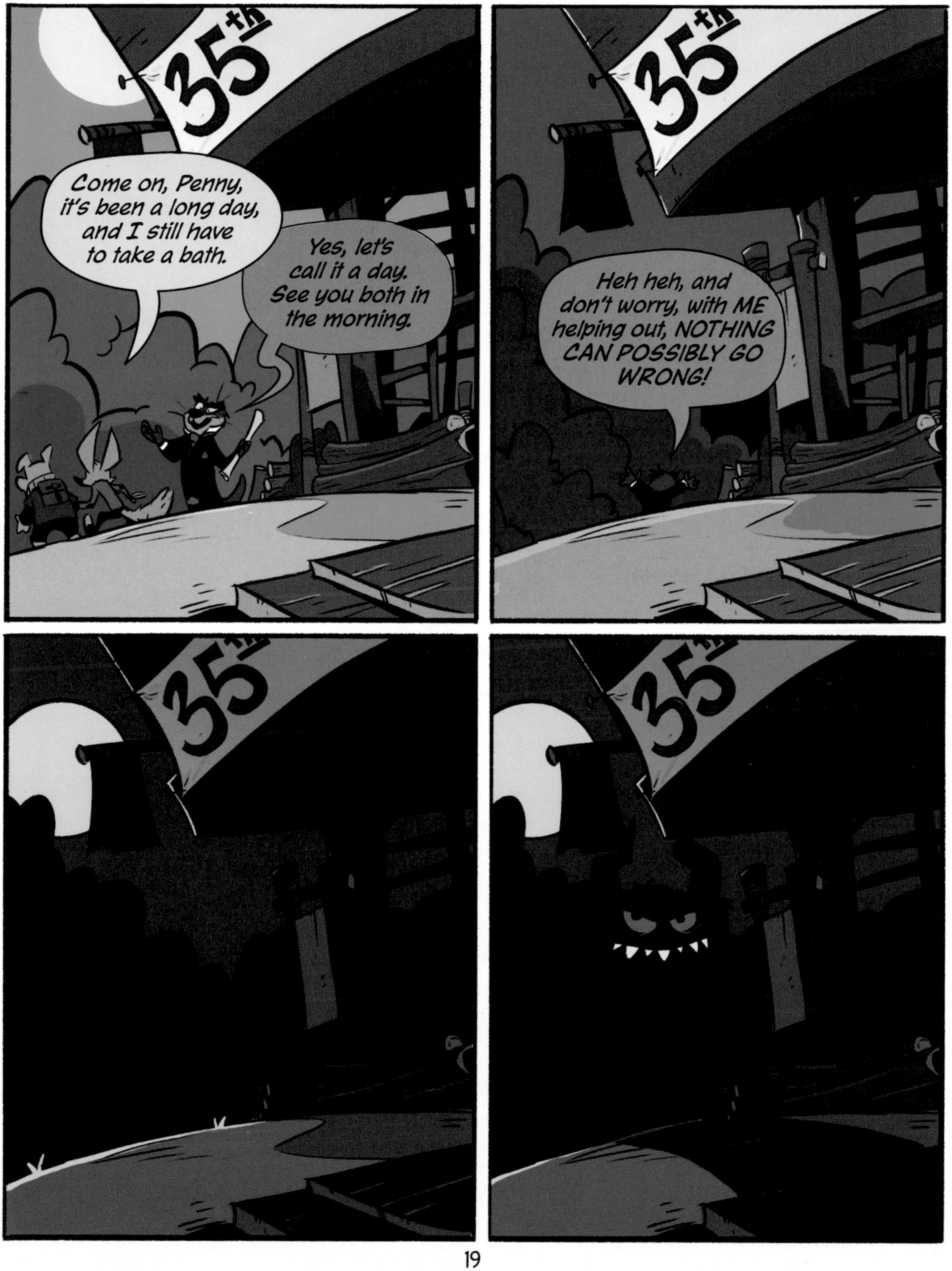
35th
Come on, Penny, it's been a long day, and I still have to take a bath.
Yes, let's call it a day. See you both in the morning.
Heh heh, and don't worry, with ME helping out, NOTHING CAN POSSIBLY GO WRONG!

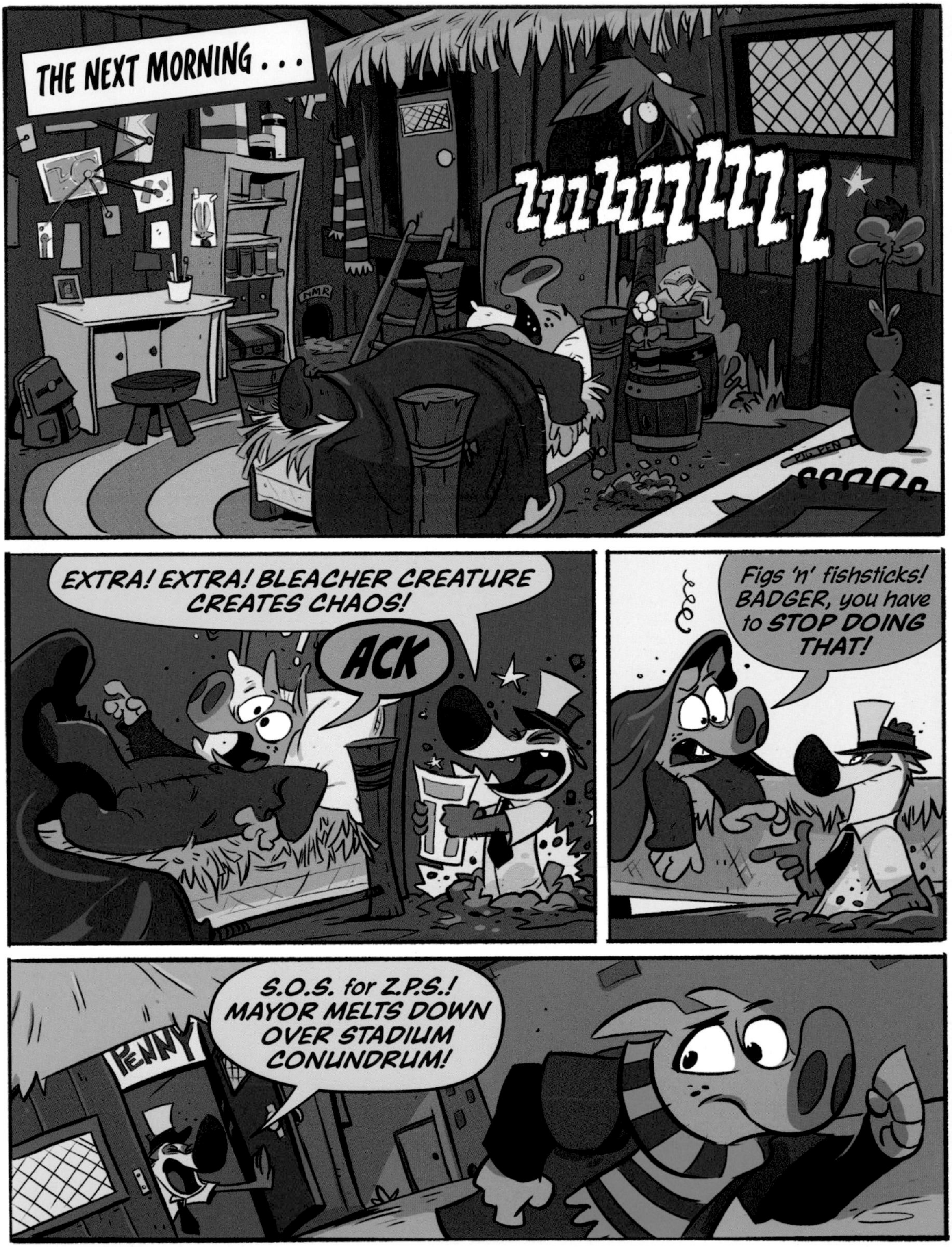
THE NEXT MORNING . . .
ZZZZZZZZZZZ Z
PIG PEN
NMR
EXTRA! EXTRA! BLEACHER CREATURE CREATES CHAOS!
ACK
Figs 'n' fishsticks! BADGER, you have to STOP DOING THAT!
S.O.S. for Z.P.S.! MAYOR MELTS DOWN OVER STADIUM CONUNDRUM!
PENNY

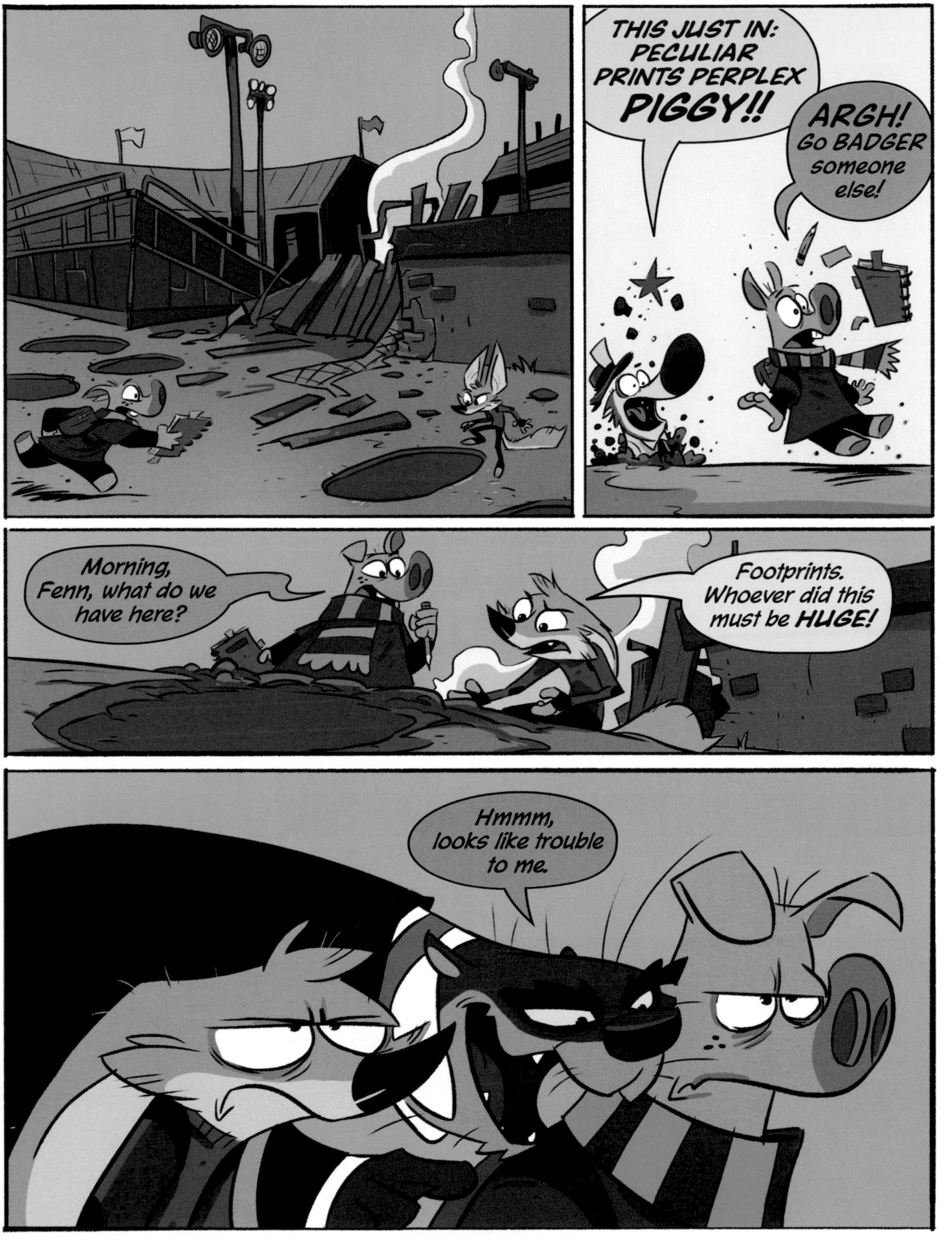
THIS JUST IN: PECULIAR PRINTS PERPLEX PIGGY!!
ARGH! Go BADGER someone else!
Morning, Fenn, what do we have here?
Footprints. Whoever did this must be HUGE!
Hmmm, looks like trouble to me.

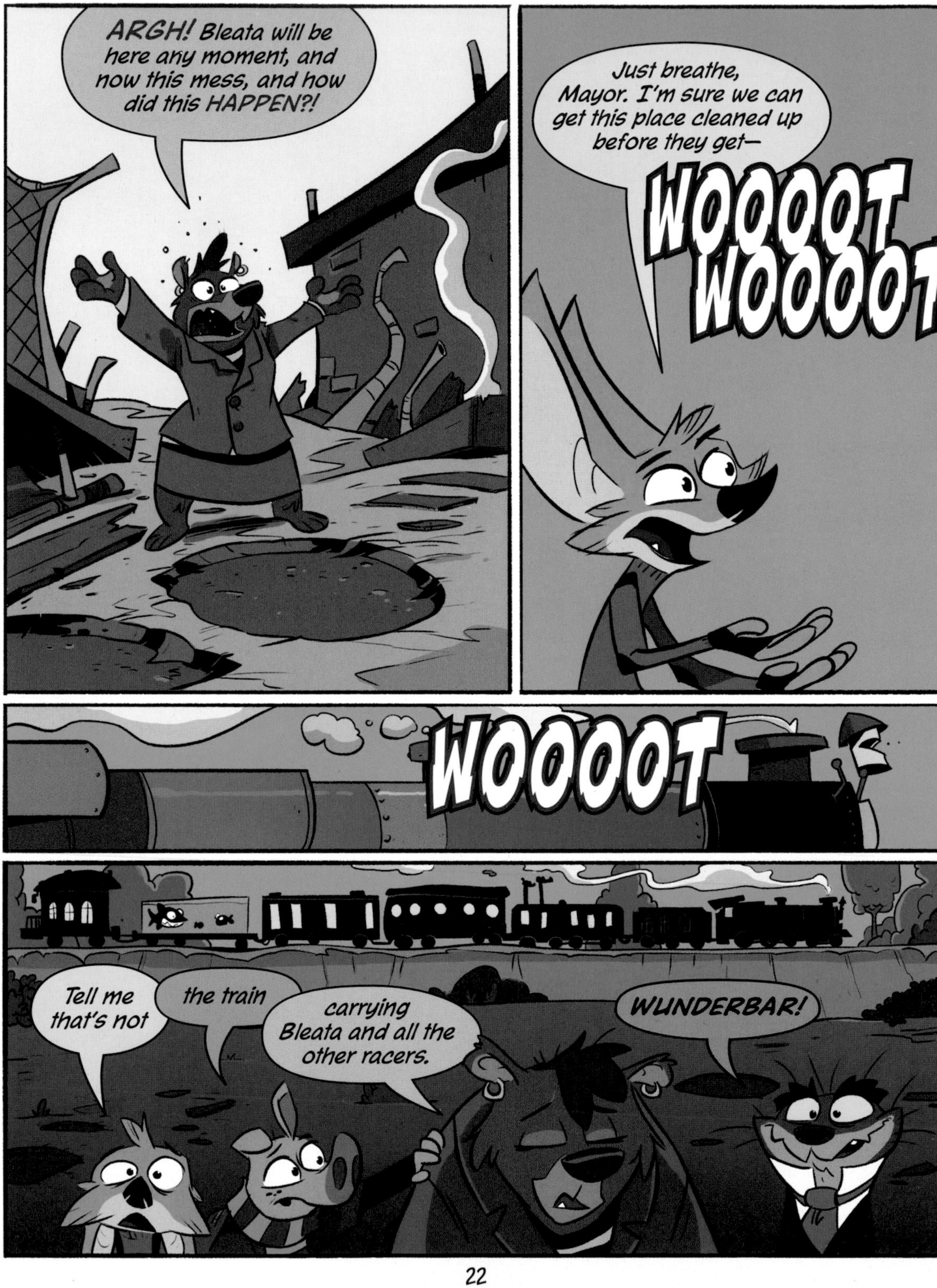
ARGH! Bleata will be here any moment, and now this mess, and how did this HAPPEN?!
Just breathe, Mayor. I'm sure we can get this place cleaned up before they get—
WOOOOT WOOOOT
WOOOOT
Tell me that's not
the train
carrying Bleata and all the other racers.
WUNDERBAR!

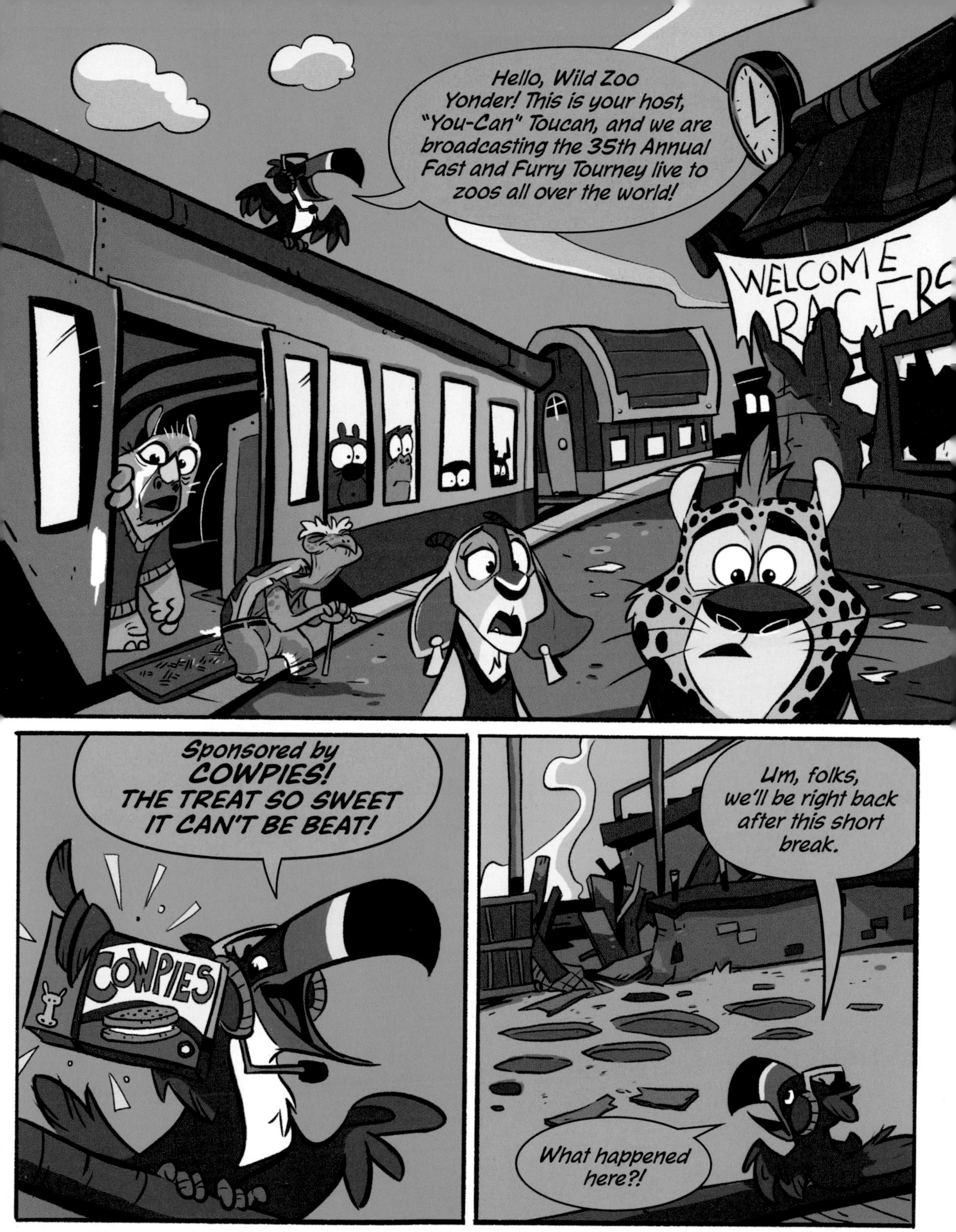
Hello, Wild Zoo Yonder! This is your host, "You-Can" Toucan, and we are broadcasting the 35th Annual Fast and Furry Tourney live to zoos all over the world!
WELCOME RACERS
Sponsored by COWPIES! THE TREAT SO SWEET IT CAN'T BE BEAT!
COWPIES
Um, folks, we'll be right back after this short break.
What happened here?!

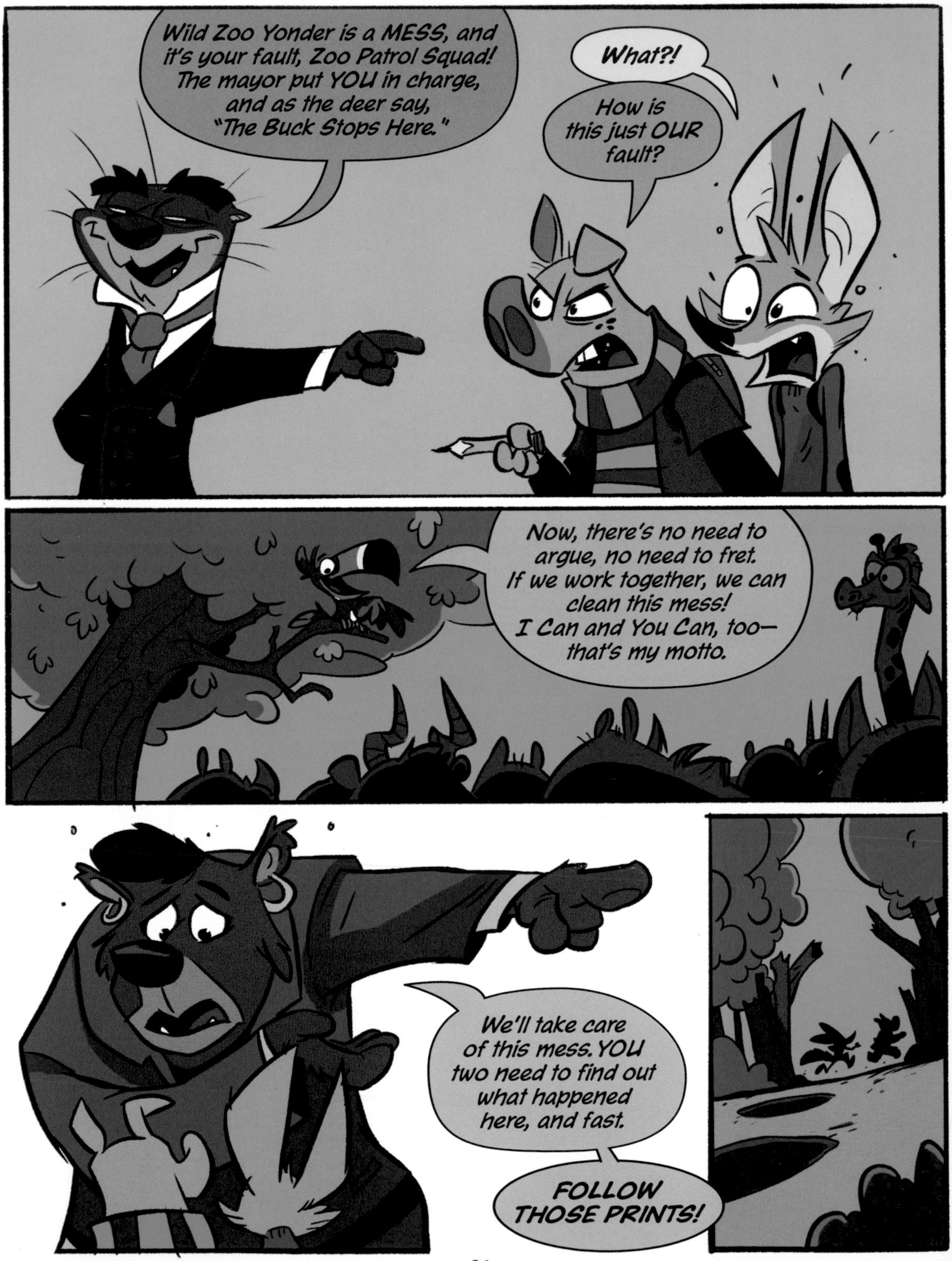
Wild Zoo Yonder is a MESS, and it's your fault, Zoo Patrol Squad! The mayor put YOU in charge, and as the deer say, "The Buck Stops Here."
What?!
How is this just OUR fault?
Now, there's no need to argue, no need to fret. If we work together, we can clean this mess! I Can and You Can, too—that's my motto.
We'll take care of this mess. YOU two need to find out what happened here, and fast.
FOLLOW THOSE PRINTS!

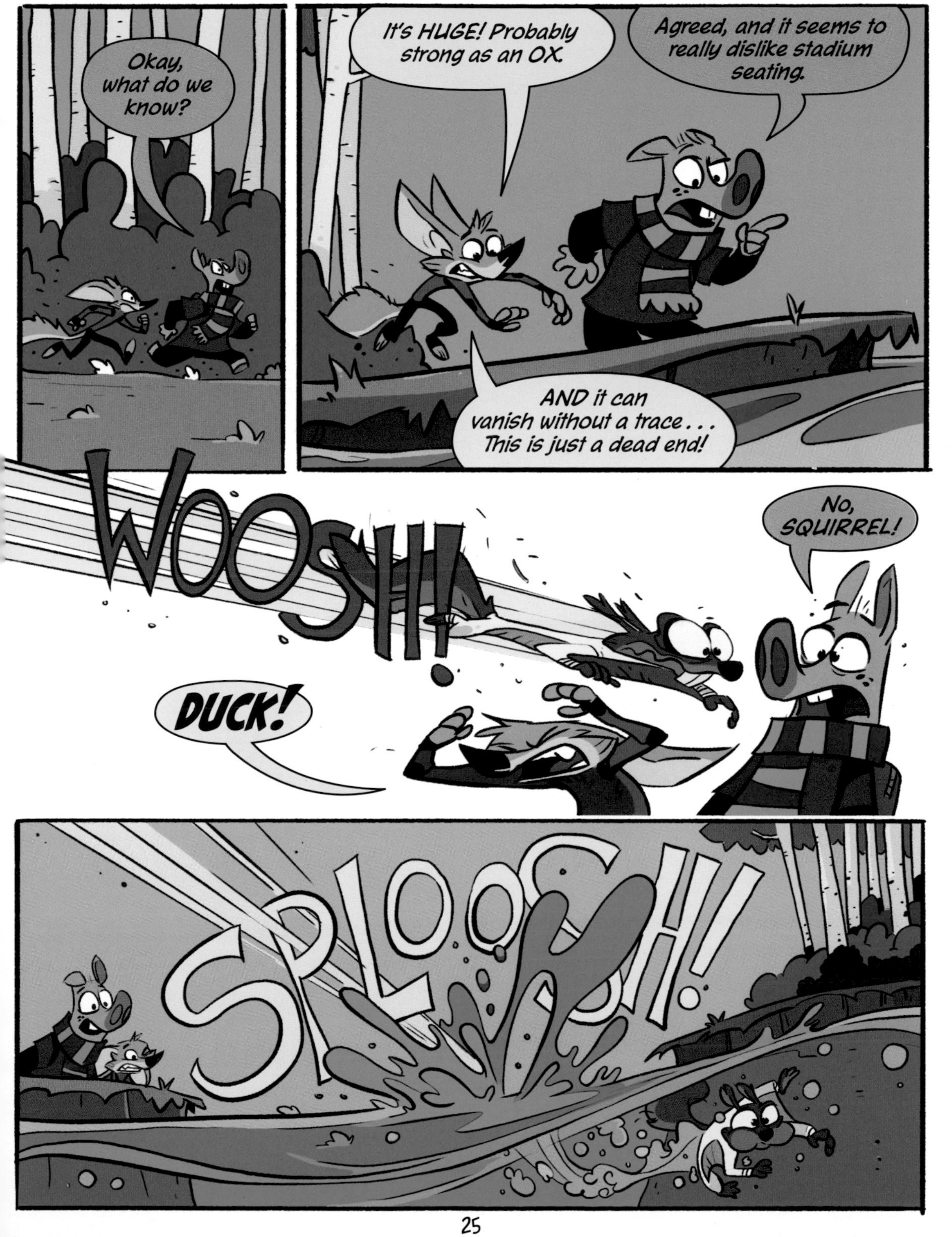
Okay, what do we know?
It's HUGE! Probably strong as an OX.
Agreed, and it seems to really dislike stadium seating.
AND it can vanish without a trace . . . This is just a dead end!
WOOSH!!
No, SQUIRREL!
DUCK!
SPLOOSH!!

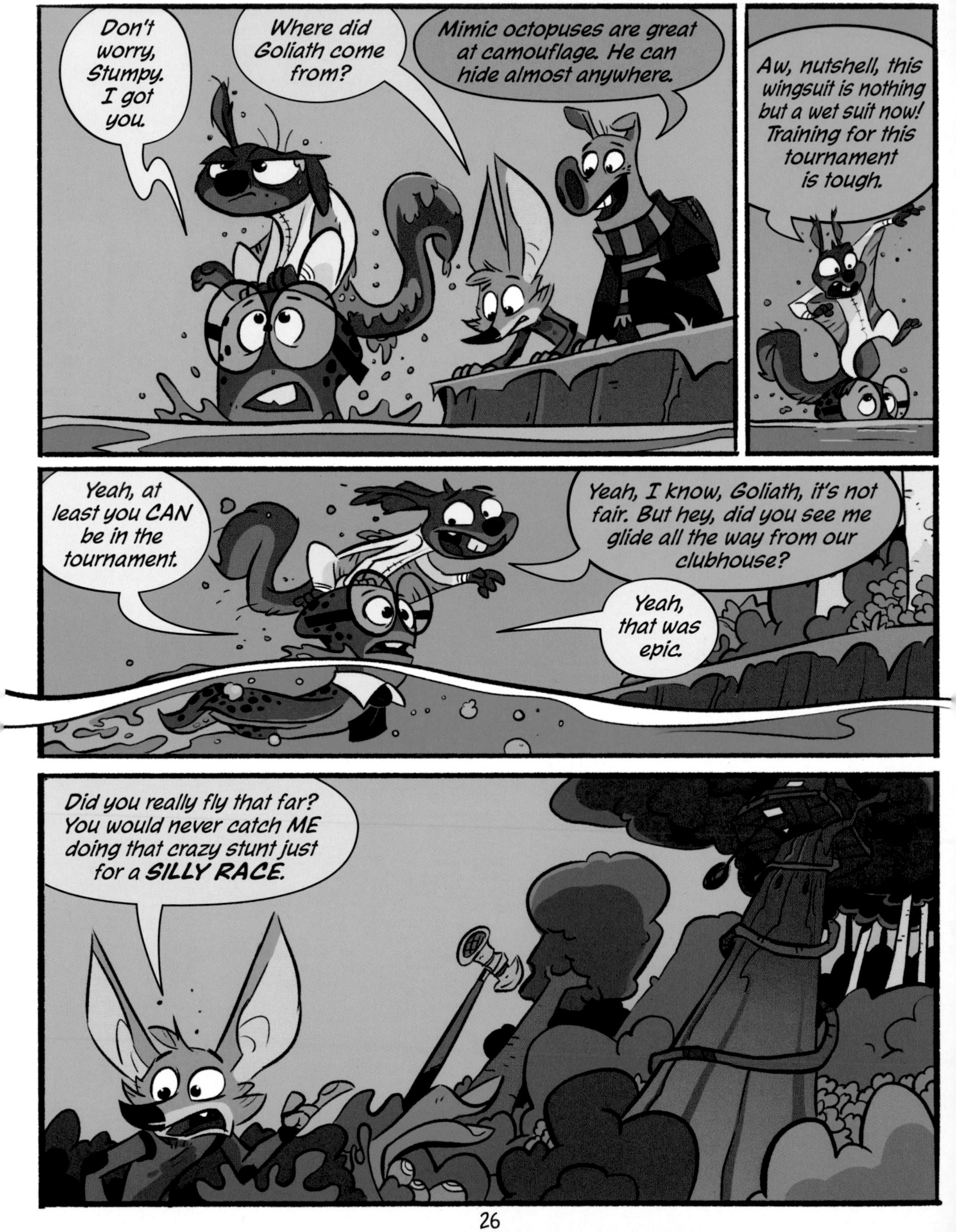
Don't worry, Stumpy. I got you.
Where did Goliath come from?
Mimic octopuses are great at camouflage. He can hide almost anywhere.
Aw, nutshell, this wingsuit is nothing but a wet suit now! Training for this tournament is tough.
Yeah, at least you CAN be in the tournament.
Yeah, I know, Goliath, it's not fair. But hey, did you see me glide all the way from our clubhouse?
Yeah, that was epic.
Did you really fly that far? You would never catch ME doing that crazy stunt just for a SILLY RACE.

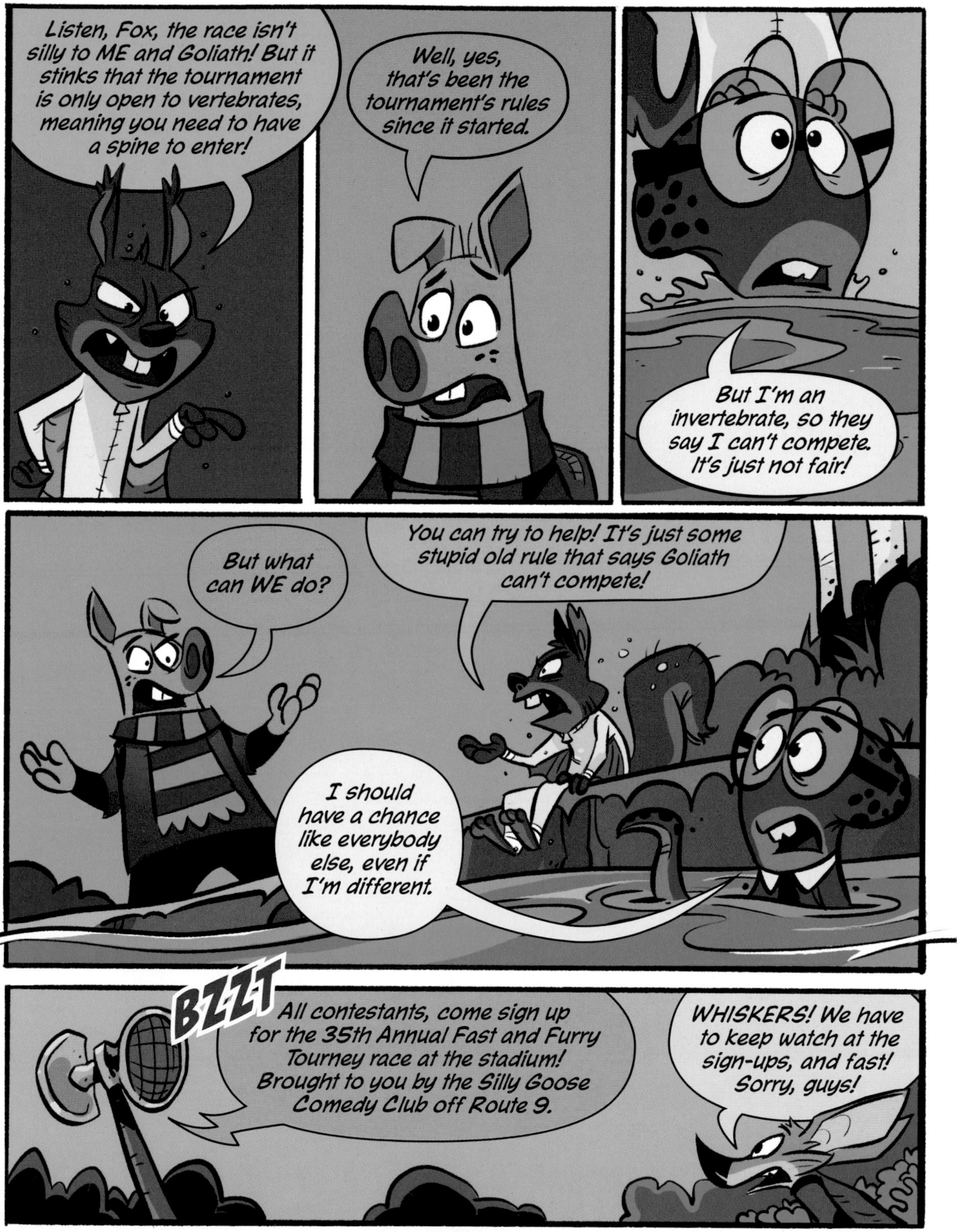
Listen, Fox, the race isn't silly to ME and Goliath! But it stinks that the tournament is only open to vertebrates, meaning you need to have a spine to enter!
Well, yes, that's been the tournament's rules since it started.
But I'm an invertebrate, so they say I can't compete. It's just not fair!
But what can WE do?
You can try to help! It's just some stupid old rule that says Goliath can't compete!
I should have a chance like everybody else, even if I'm different.
BZZT
All contestants, come sign up for the 35th Annual Fast and Furry Tourney race at the stadium! Brought to you by the Silly Goose Comedy Club off Route 9.
WHISKERS! We have to keep watch at the sign-ups, and fast! Sorry, guys!

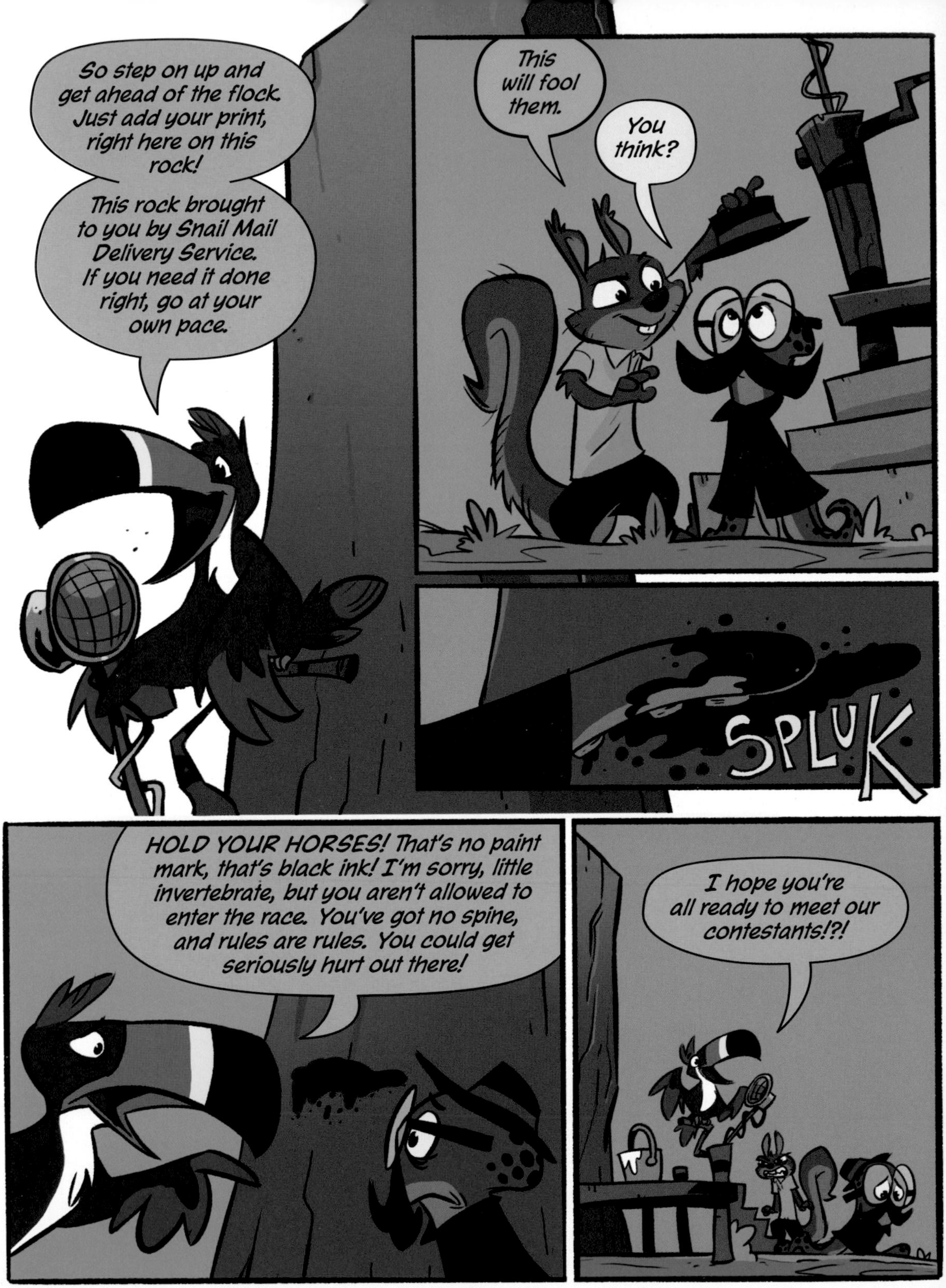
So step on up and get ahead of the flock. Just add your print, right here on this rock!
This rock brought to you by Snail Mail Delivery Service. If you need it done right, go at your own pace.
This will fool them.
You think?
SPLUK
HOLD YOUR HORSES! That's no paint mark, that's black ink! I'm sorry, little invertebrate, but you aren't allowed to enter the race. You've got no spine, and rules are rules. You could get seriously hurt out there!
I hope you're all ready to meet our contestants!?!

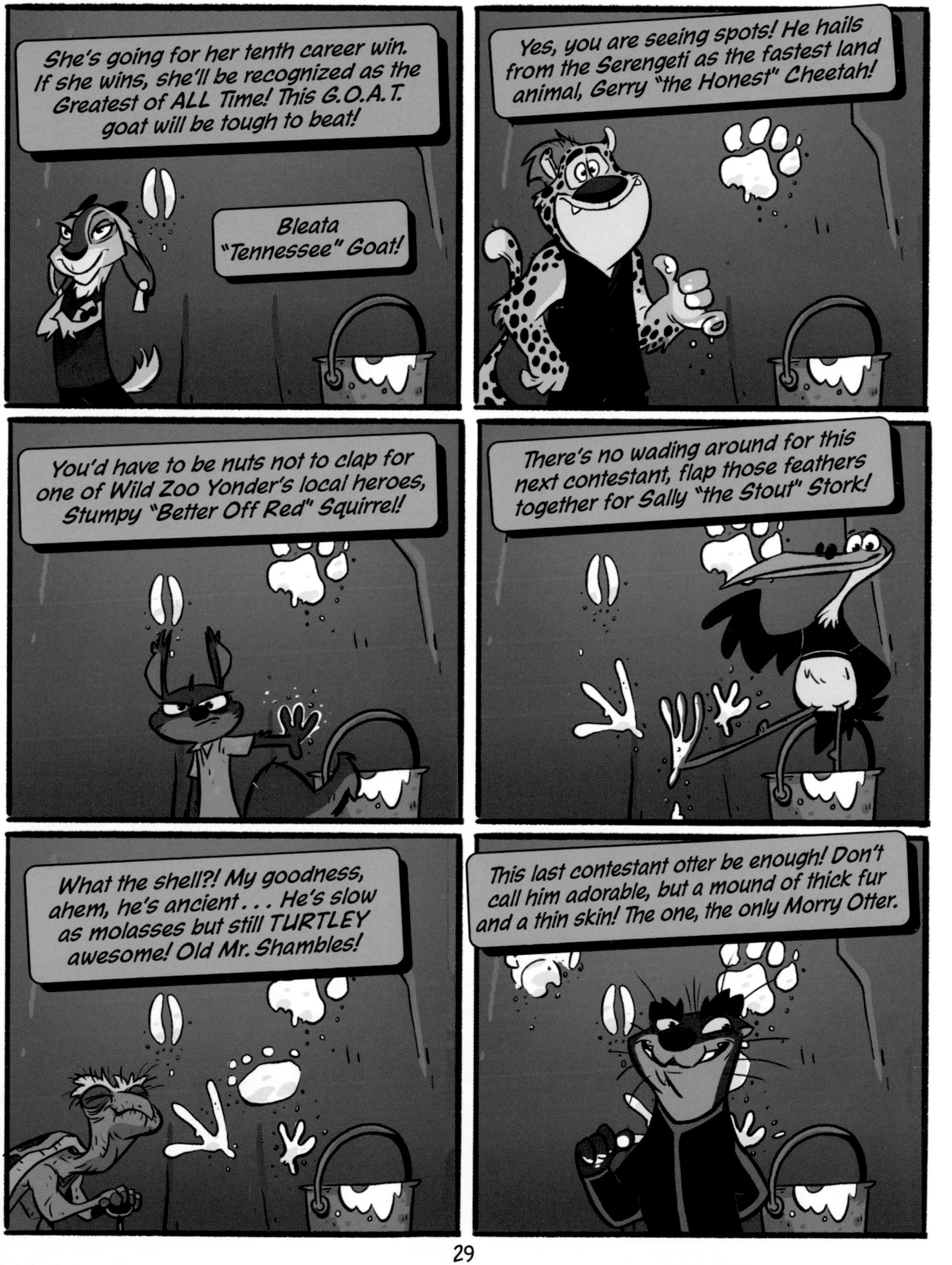
She's going for her tenth career win. If she wins, she'll be recognized as the Greatest of ALL Time! This G.O.A.T. goat will be tough to beat!
Bleata "Tennessee" Goat!
Yes, you are seeing spots! He hails from the Serengeti as the fastest land animal, Gerry "the Honest" Cheetah!
You'd have to be nuts not to clap for one of Wild Zoo Yonder's local heroes, Stumpy "Better Off Red" Squirrel!
There's no wading around for this next contestant, flap those feathers together for Sally "the Stout" Stork!
What the shell?! My goodness, ahem, he's ancient . . . He's slow as molasses but still TURTLEY awesome! Old Mr. Shambles!
This last contestant otter be enough! Don't call him adorable, but a mound of thick fur and a thin skin! The one, the only Morry Otter.

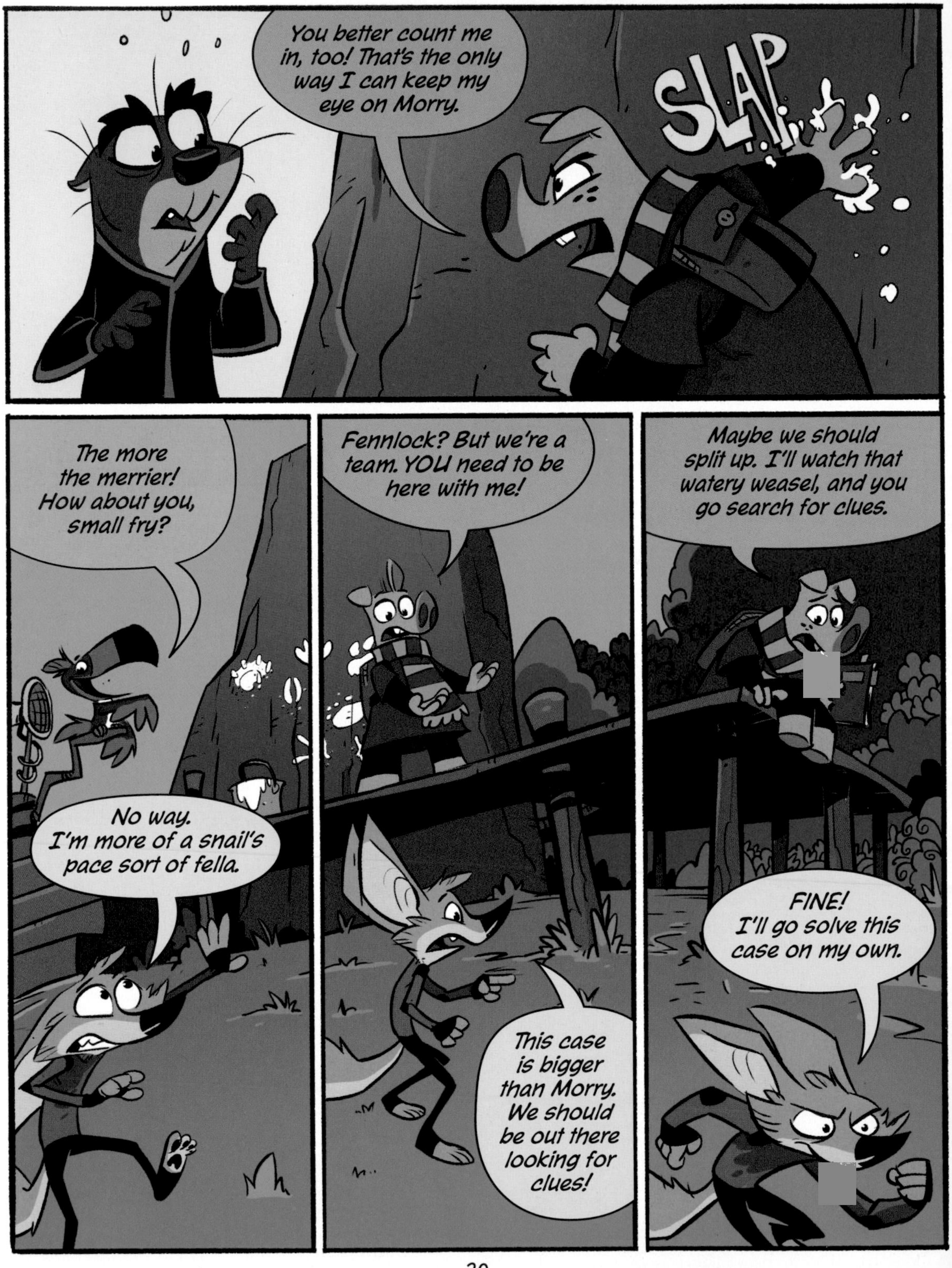
You better count me in, too! That's the only way I can keep my eye on Morry.
SLAP
The more the merrier! How about you, small fry?
No way. I'm more of a snail's pace sort of fella.
Fennlock? But we're a team. YOU need to be here with me!
This case is bigger than Morry. We should be out there looking for clues!
Maybe we should split up. I'll watch that watery weasel, and you go search for clues.
FINE! I'll go solve this case on my own.

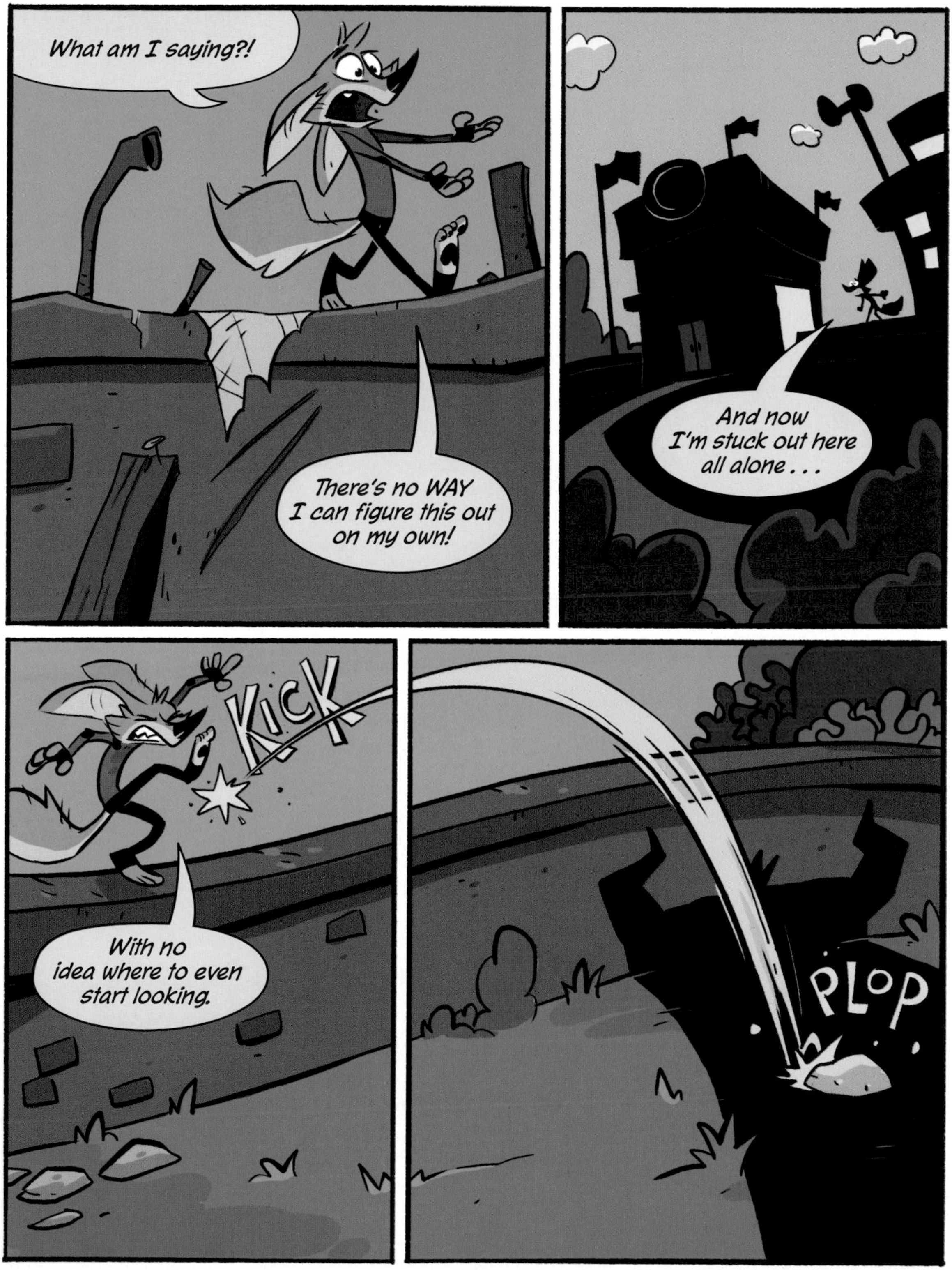
What am I saying?!
There's no WAY I can figure this out on my own!
And now I'm stuck out here all alone . . .
KICK
With no idea where to even start looking.
PLOP

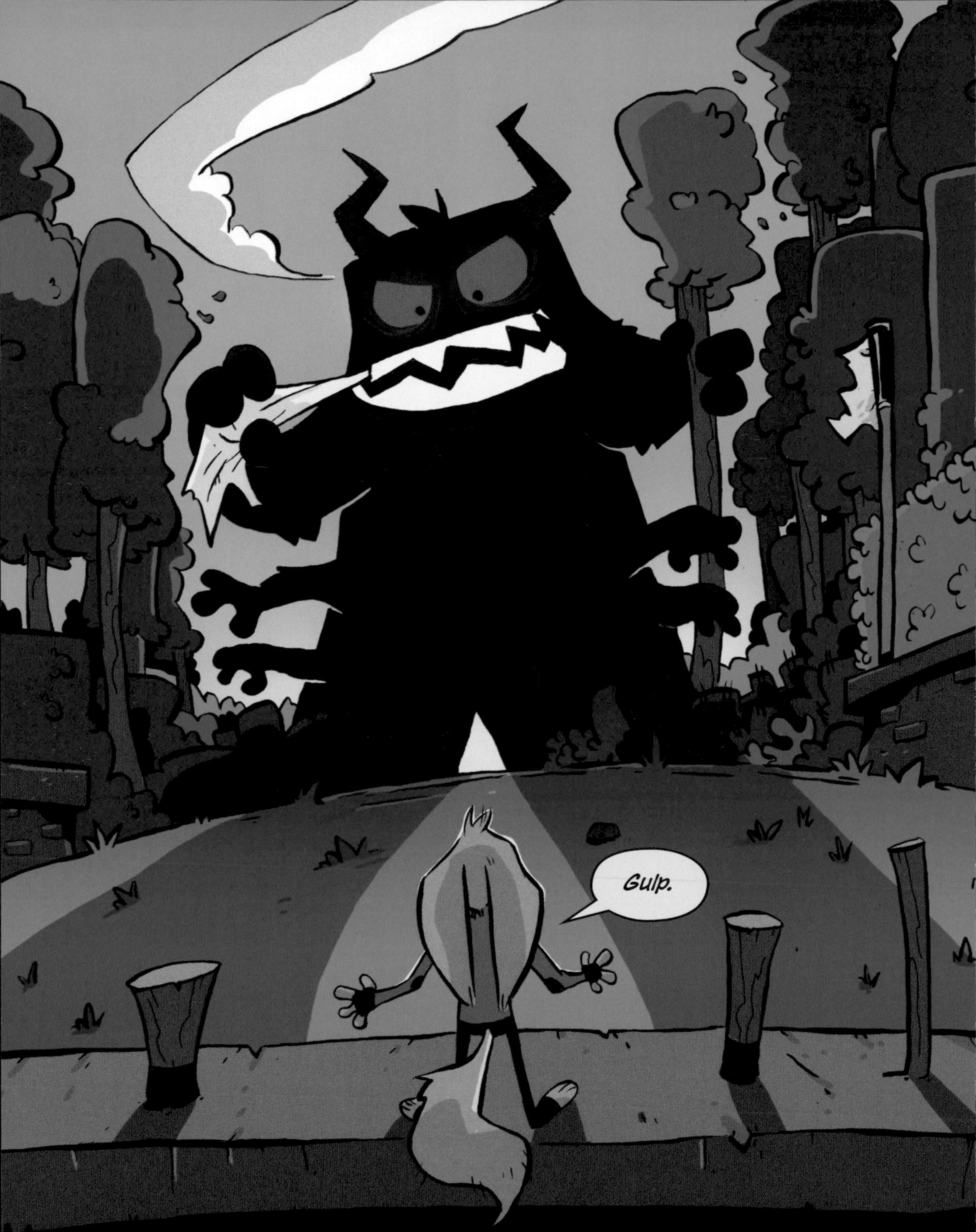
Gulp.

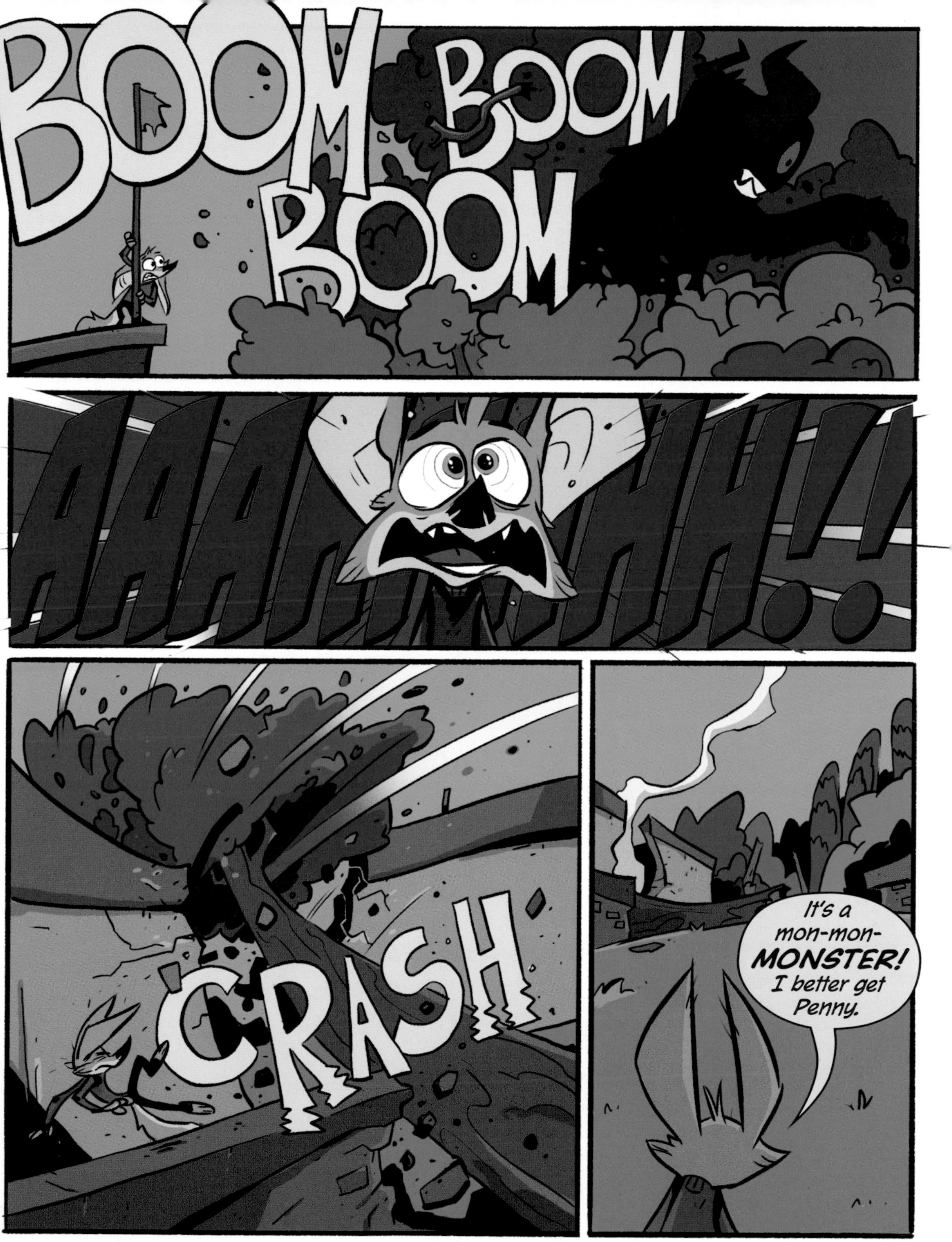
BOOM
BOOM
BOOM
AAAAAAAHH!!
CRASH
It's a mon-mon-**MONSTER!** I better get Penny.

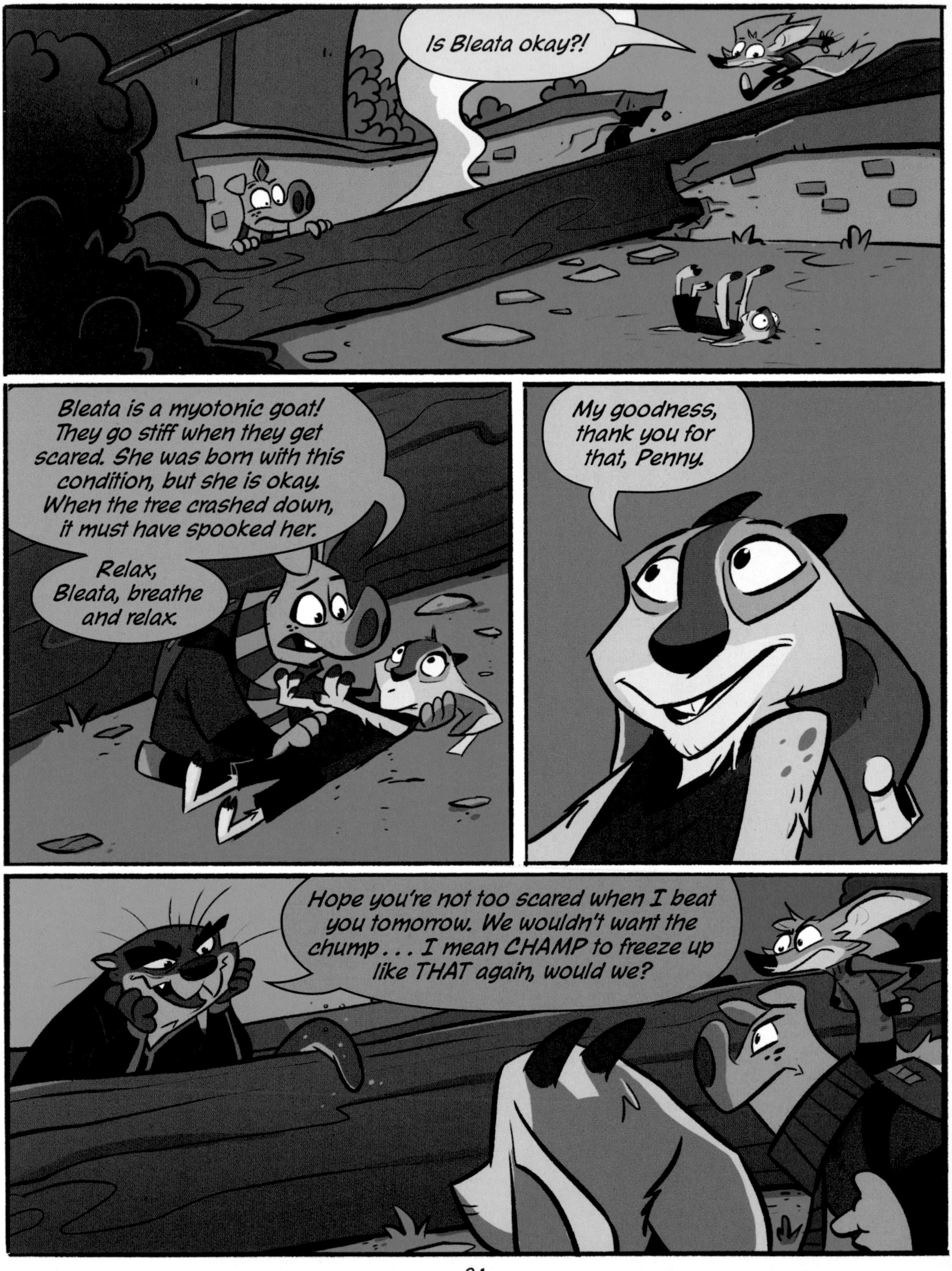
Is Bleata okay?!
Bleata is a myotonic goat! They go stiff when they get scared. She was born with this condition, but she is okay. When the tree crashed down, it must have spooked her.
Relax, Bleata, breathe and relax.
My goodness, thank you for that, Penny.
Hope you're not too scared when I beat you tomorrow. We wouldn't want the chump . . . I mean CHAMP to freeze up like THAT again, would we?

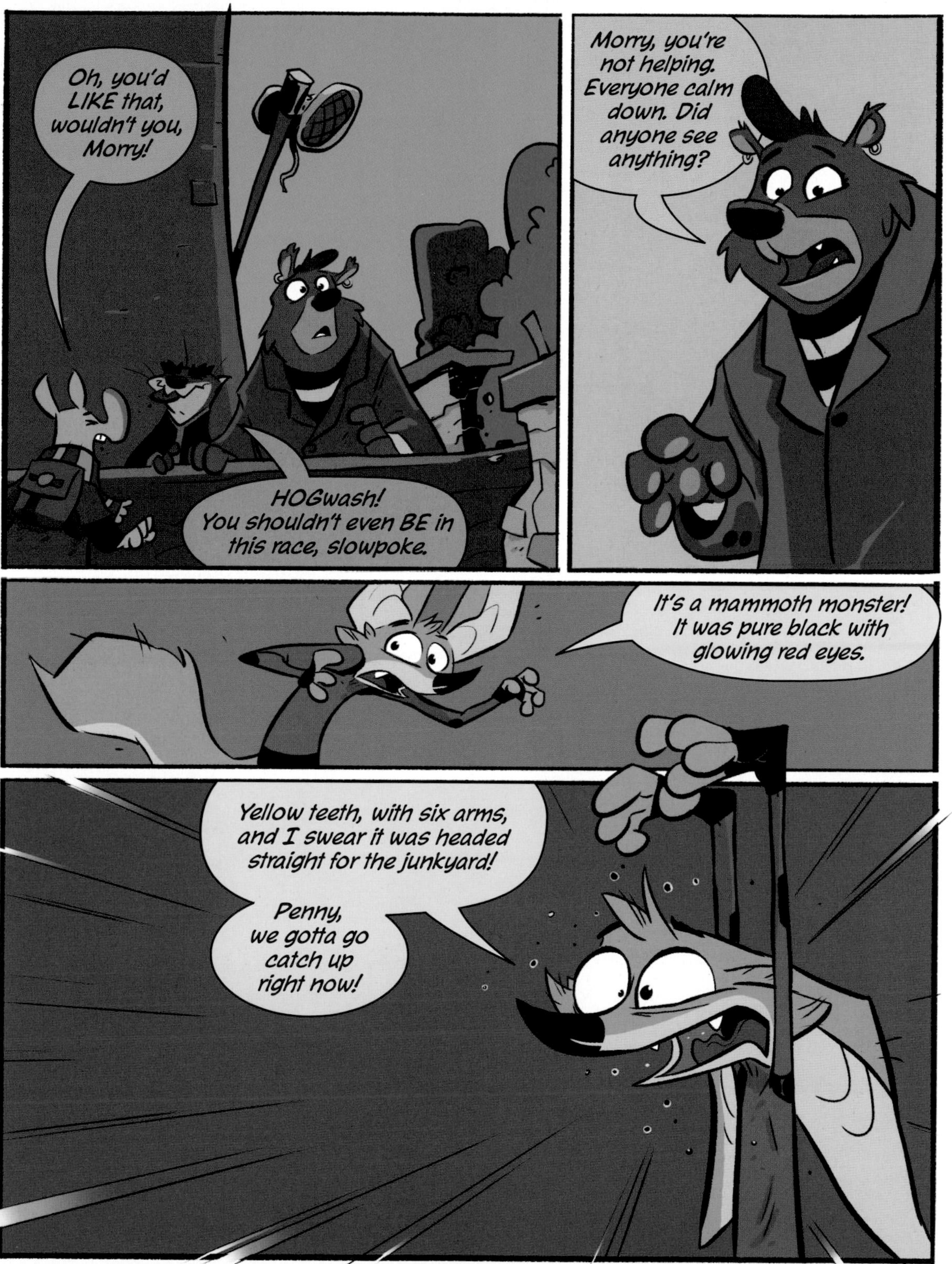
Oh, you'd LIKE that, wouldn't you, Morry!
HOGwash! You shouldn't even BE in this race, slowpoke.
Morry, you're not helping. Everyone calm down. Did anyone see anything?
It's a mammoth monster! It was pure black with glowing red eyes.
Yellow teeth, with six arms, and I swear it was headed straight for the junkyard!
Penny, we gotta go catch up right now!

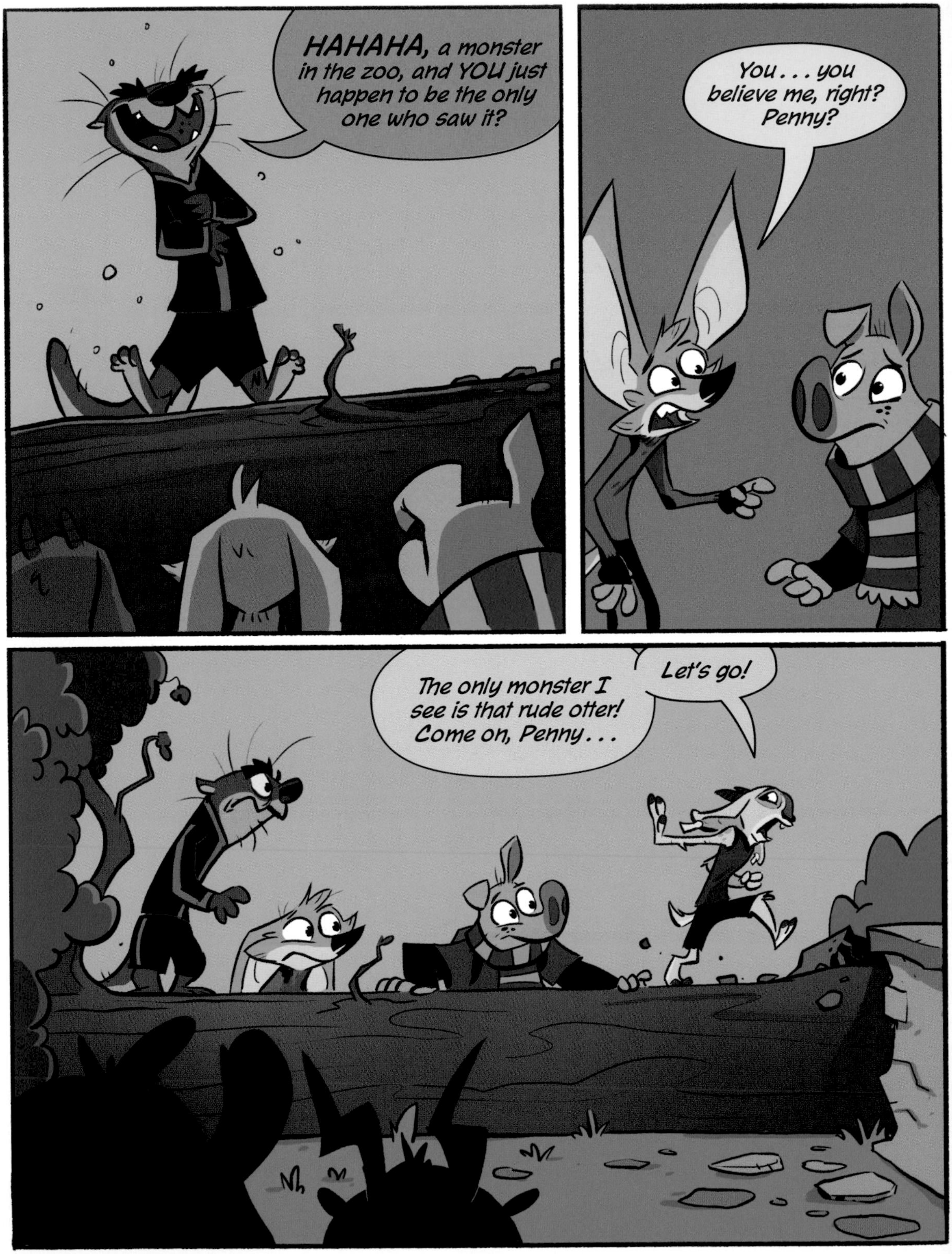
HAHAHA, a monster in the zoo, and YOU just happen to be the only one who saw it?
You . . . you believe me, right? Penny?
The only monster I see is that rude otter! Come on, Penny . . .
Let's go!

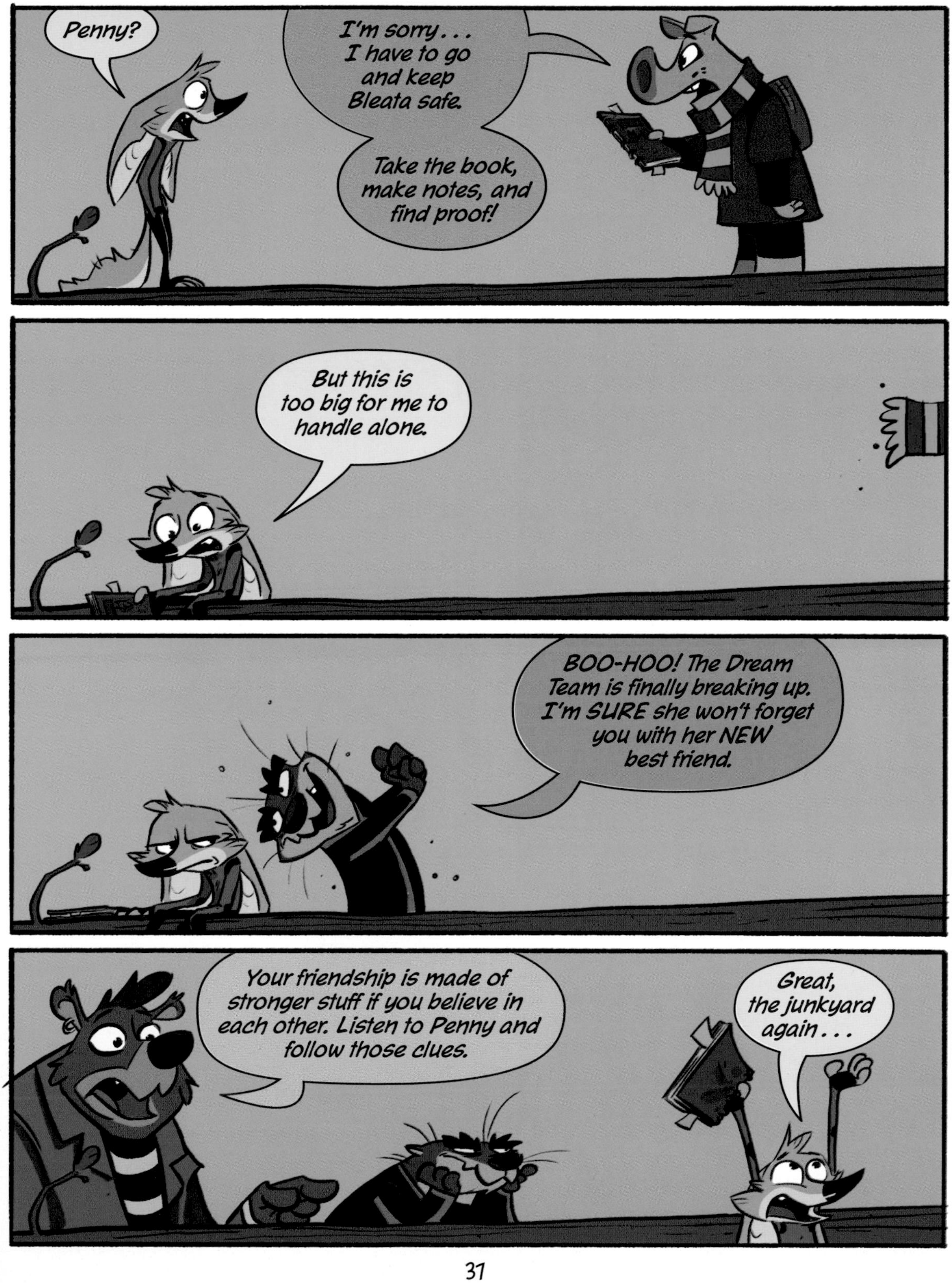
Penny?
I'm sorry . . . I have to go and keep Bleata safe.
Take the book, make notes, and find proof!
But this is too big for me to handle alone.
BOO-HOO! The Dream Team is finally breaking up. I'm SURE she won't forget you with her NEW best friend.
Your friendship is made of stronger stuff if you believe in each other. Listen to Penny and follow those clues.
Great, the junkyard again . . .

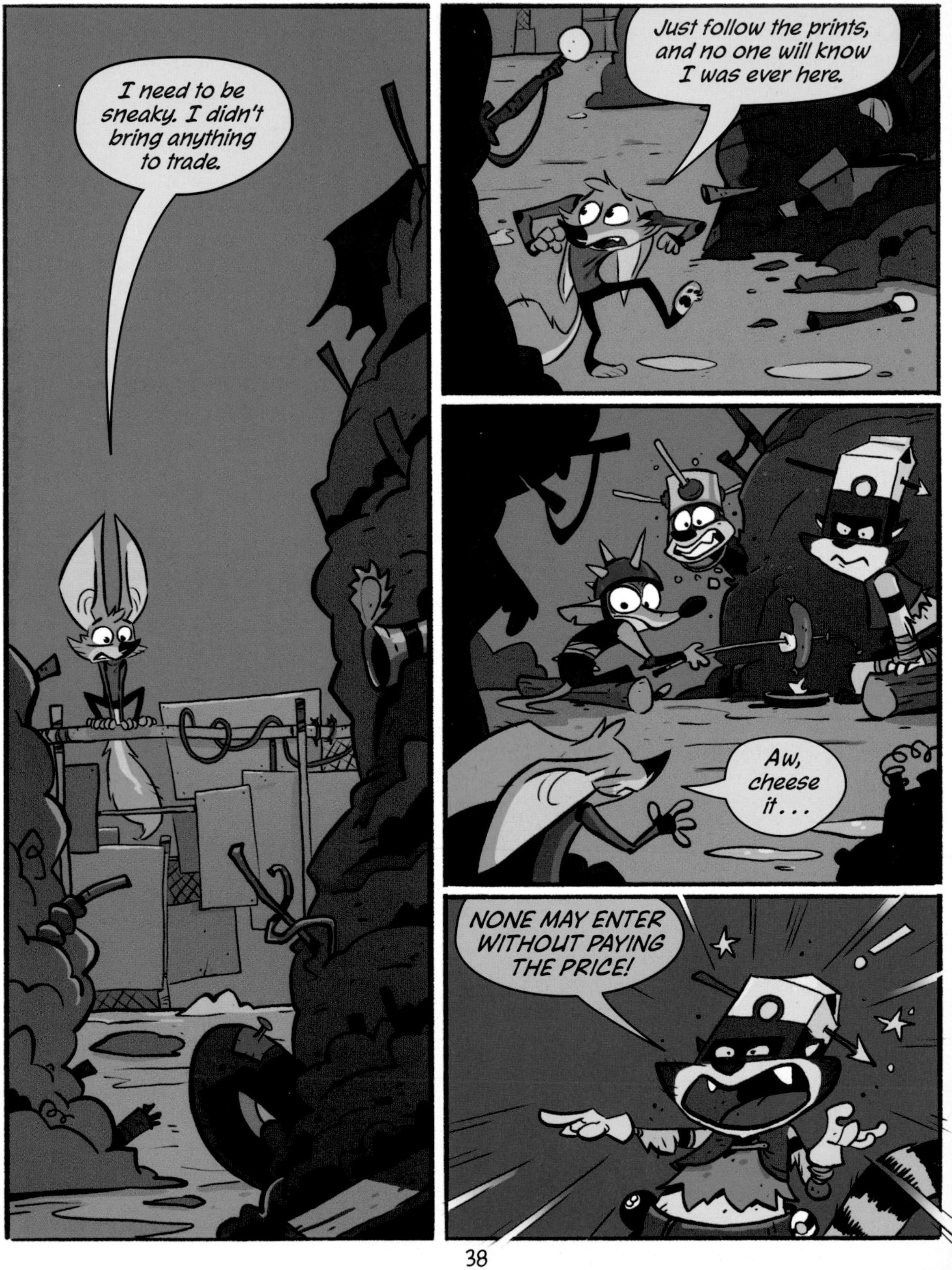
I need to be sneaky. I didn't bring anything to trade.
Just follow the prints, and no one will know I was ever here.
Aw, cheese it...
NONE MAY ENTER WITHOUT PAYING THE PRICE!

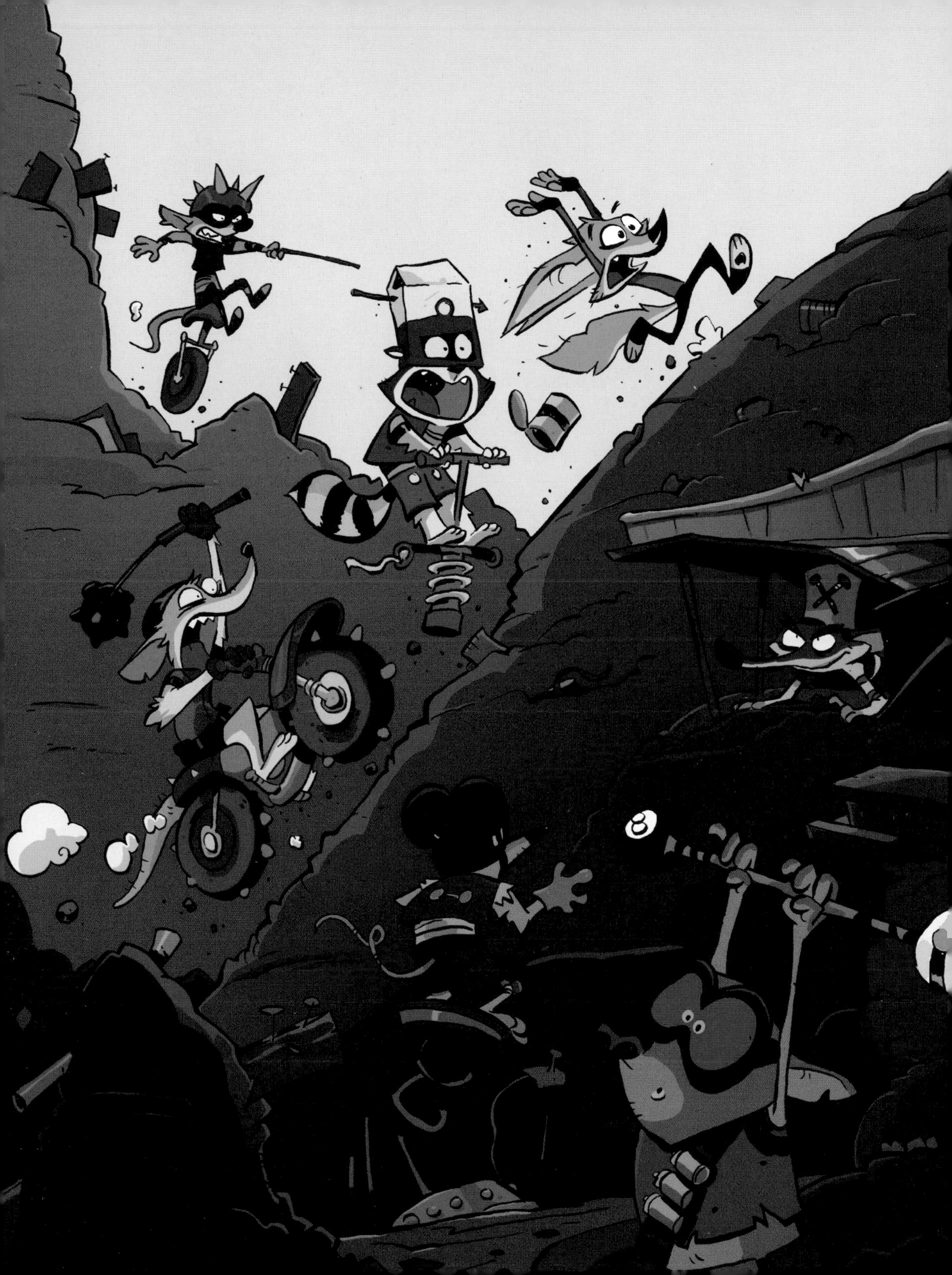

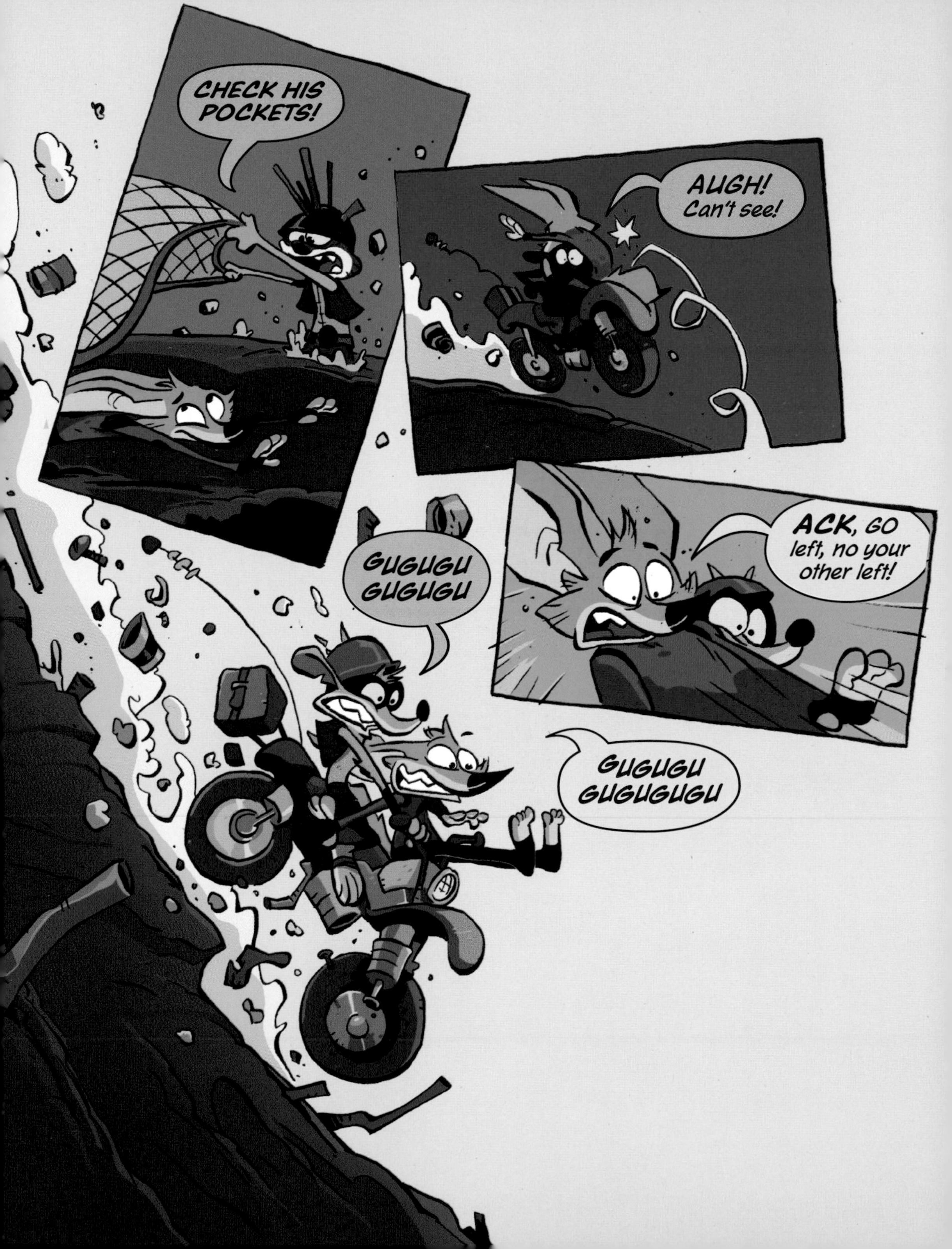
CHECK HIS POCKETS!
AUGH! Can't see!
ACK, GO left, no your other left!
GUGUGU GUGUGU
GUGUGU GUGUGUGU

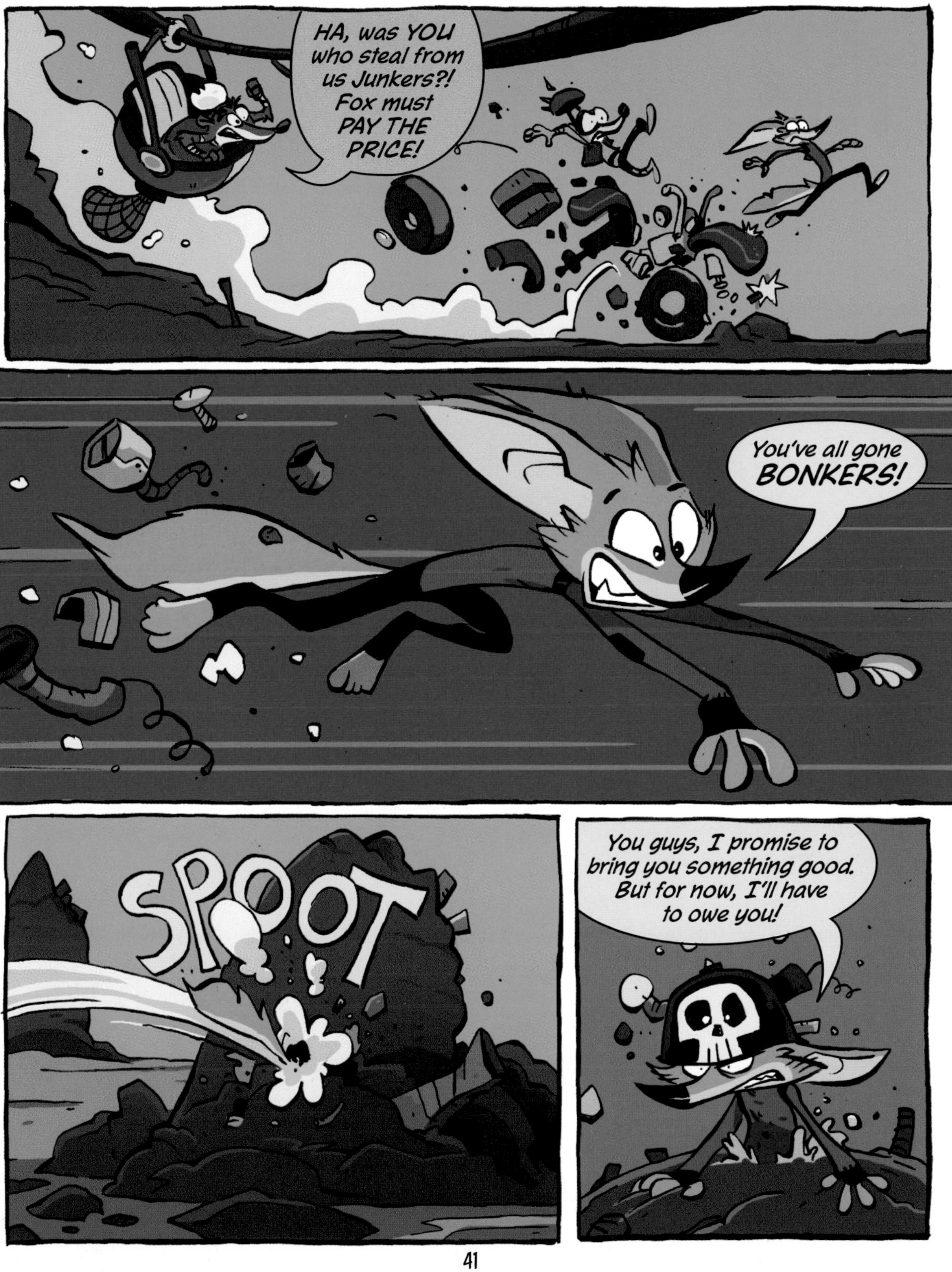
HA, was YOU who steal from us Junkers?! Fox must PAY THE PRICE!
You've all gone BONKERS!
SPOOT
You guys, I promise to bring you something good. But for now, I'll have to owe you!

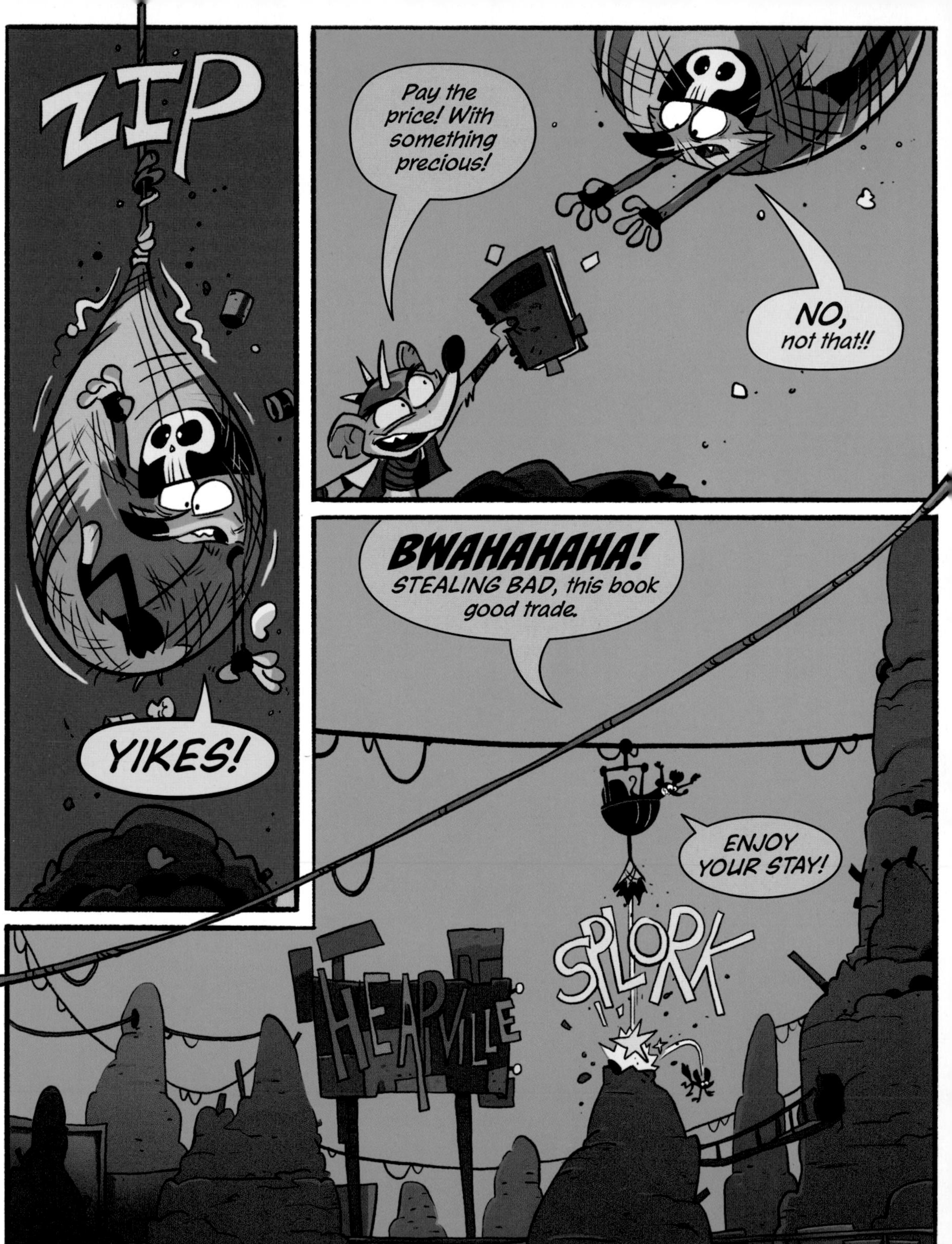
ZIP
YIKES!
Pay the price! With something precious!
NO, not that!!
BWAHAHAHA! STEALING BAD, this book good trade.
ENJOY YOUR STAY!
HEAPVILLE
SPLORK

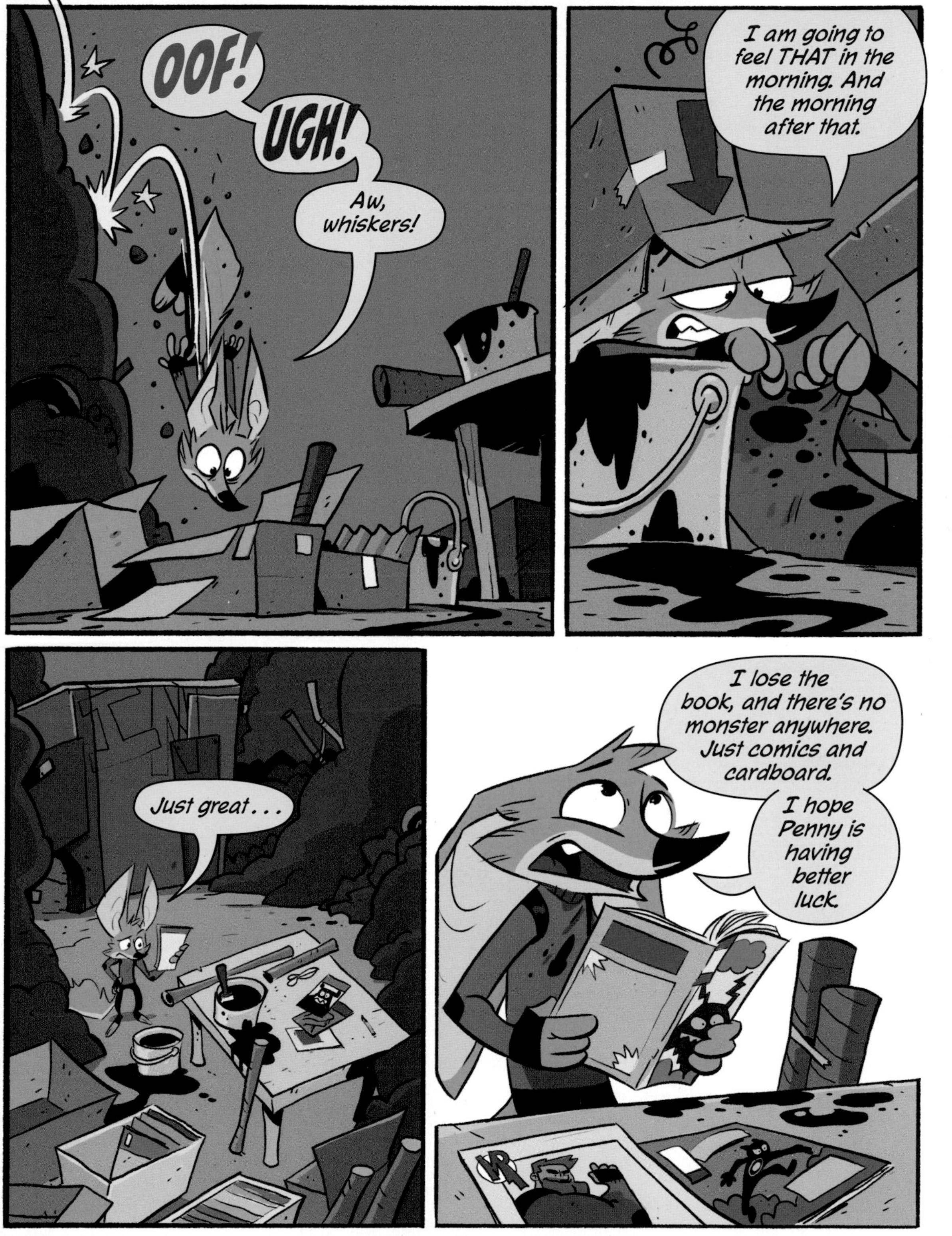
OOF!
UGH!
Aw, whiskers!
I am going to feel THAT in the morning. And the morning after that.
Just great . . .
I lose the book, and there's no monster anywhere. Just comics and cardboard.
I hope Penny is having better luck.

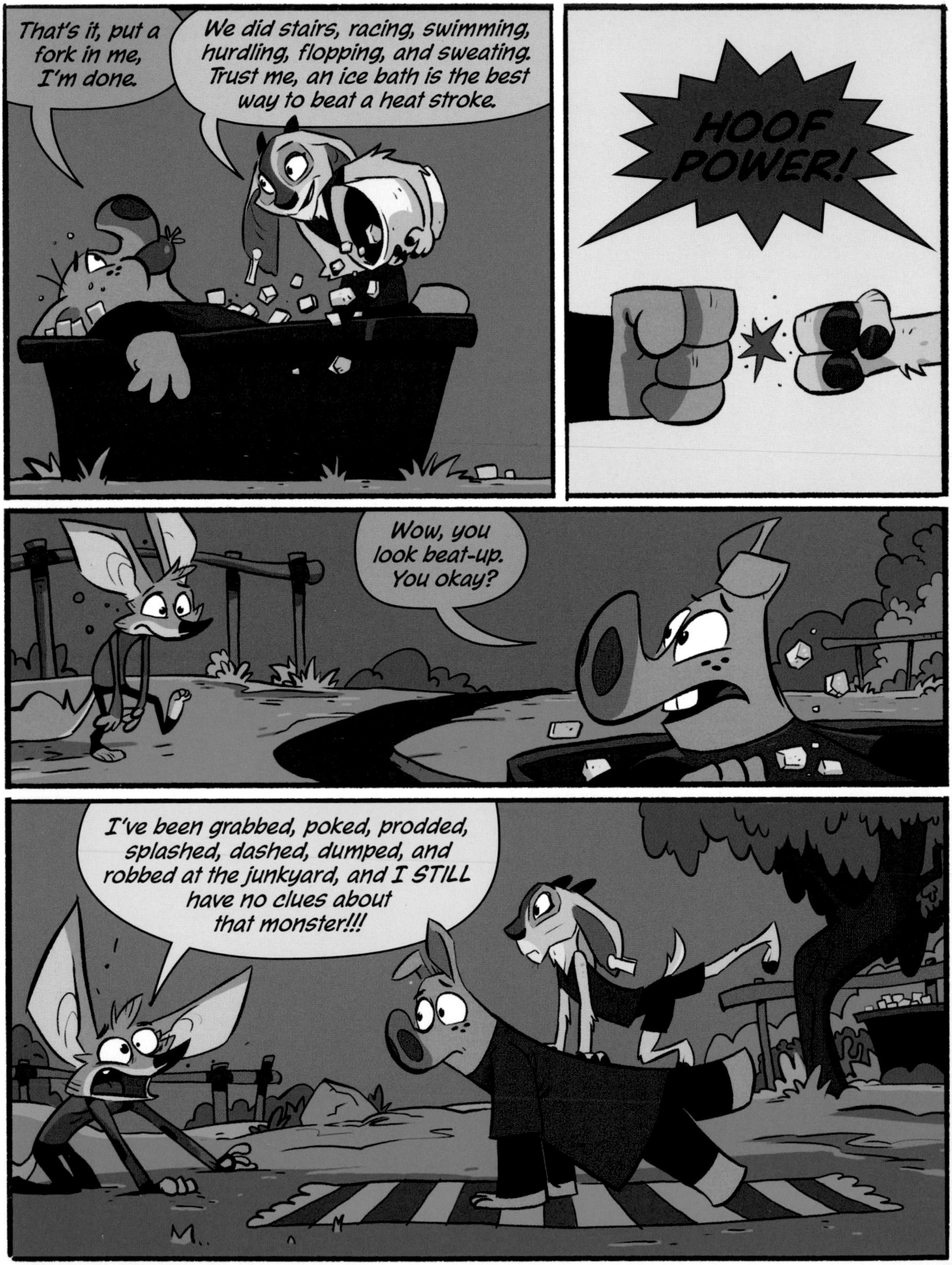
That's it, put a fork in me, I'm done.
We did stairs, racing, swimming, hurdling, flopping, and sweating. Trust me, an ice bath is the best way to beat a heat stroke.
HOOF POWER!
Wow, you look beat-up. You okay?
I've been grabbed, poked, prodded, splashed, dashed, dumped, and robbed at the junkyard, and I STILL have no clues about that monster!!!

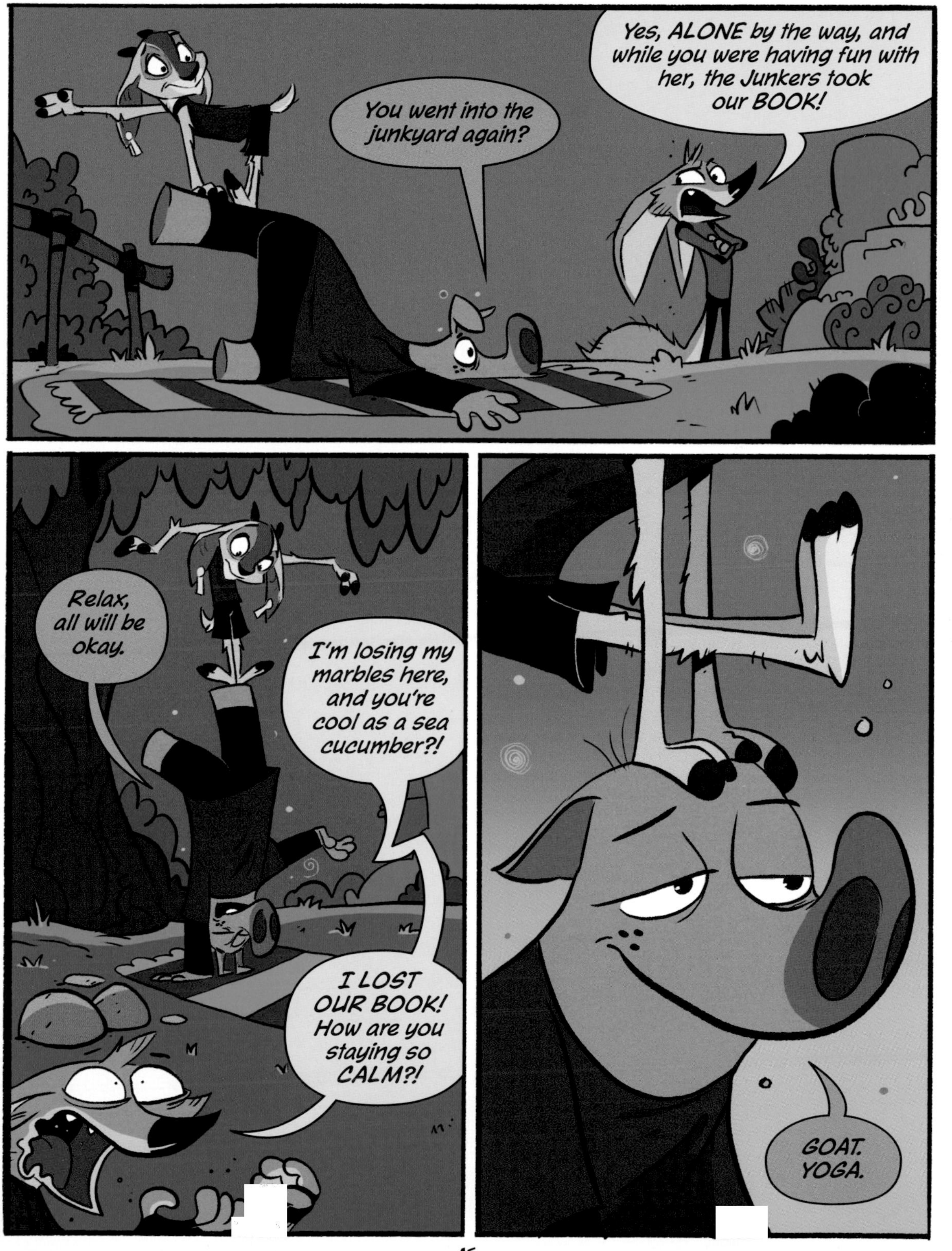
You went into the junkyard again?
Yes, ALONE by the way, and while you were having fun with her, the Junkers took our BOOK!
Relax, all will be okay.
I'm losing my marbles here, and you're cool as a sea cucumber?!
I LOST OUR BOOK! How are you staying so CALM?!
GOAT. YOGA.

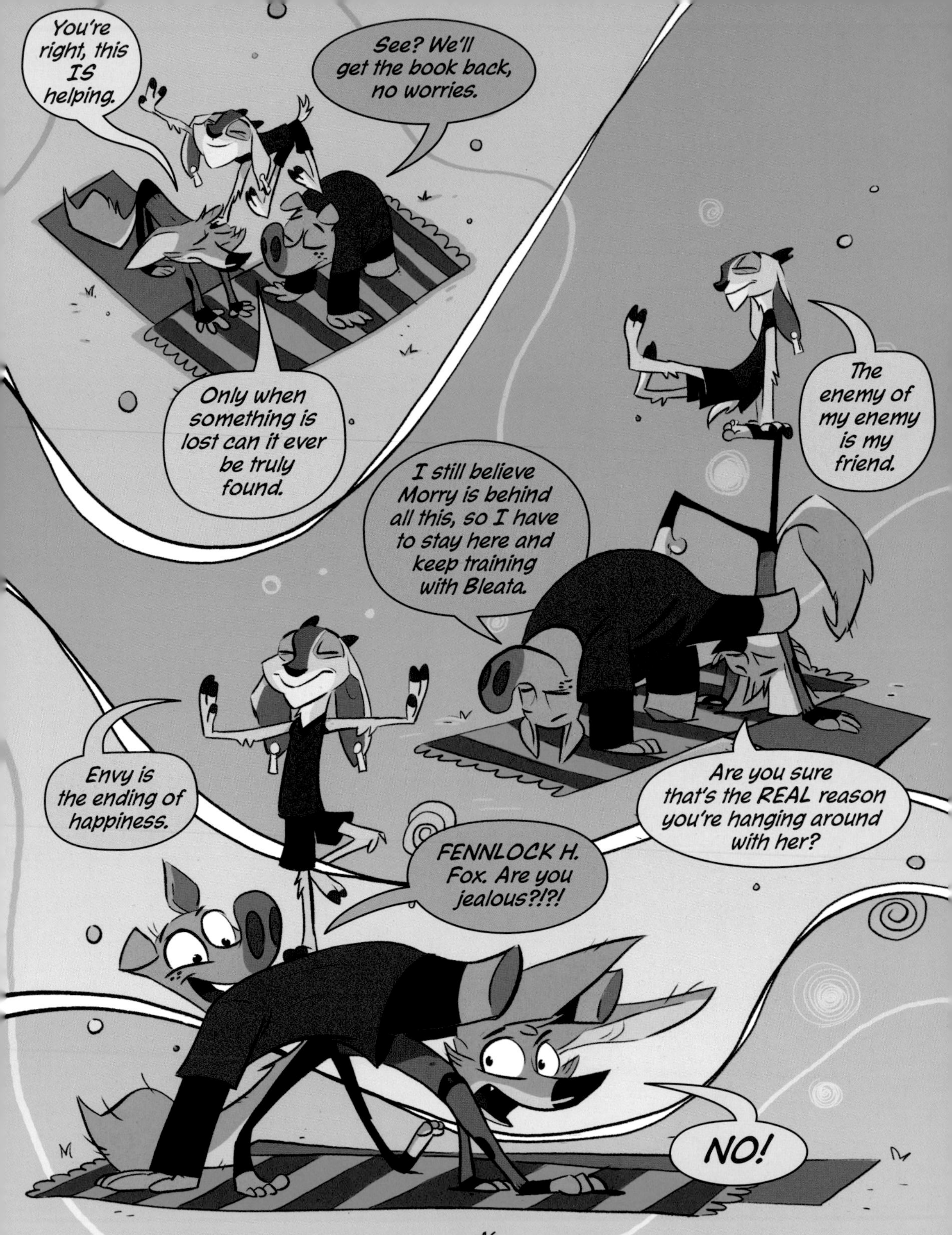
You're right, this IS helping.
See? We'll get the book back, no worries.
Only when something is lost can it ever be truly found.
The enemy of my enemy is my friend.
I still believe Morry is behind all this, so I have to stay here and keep training with Bleata.
Envy is the ending of happiness.
Are you sure that's the REAL reason you're hanging around with her?
FENNLOCK H. Fox. Are you jealous?!?!
NO!

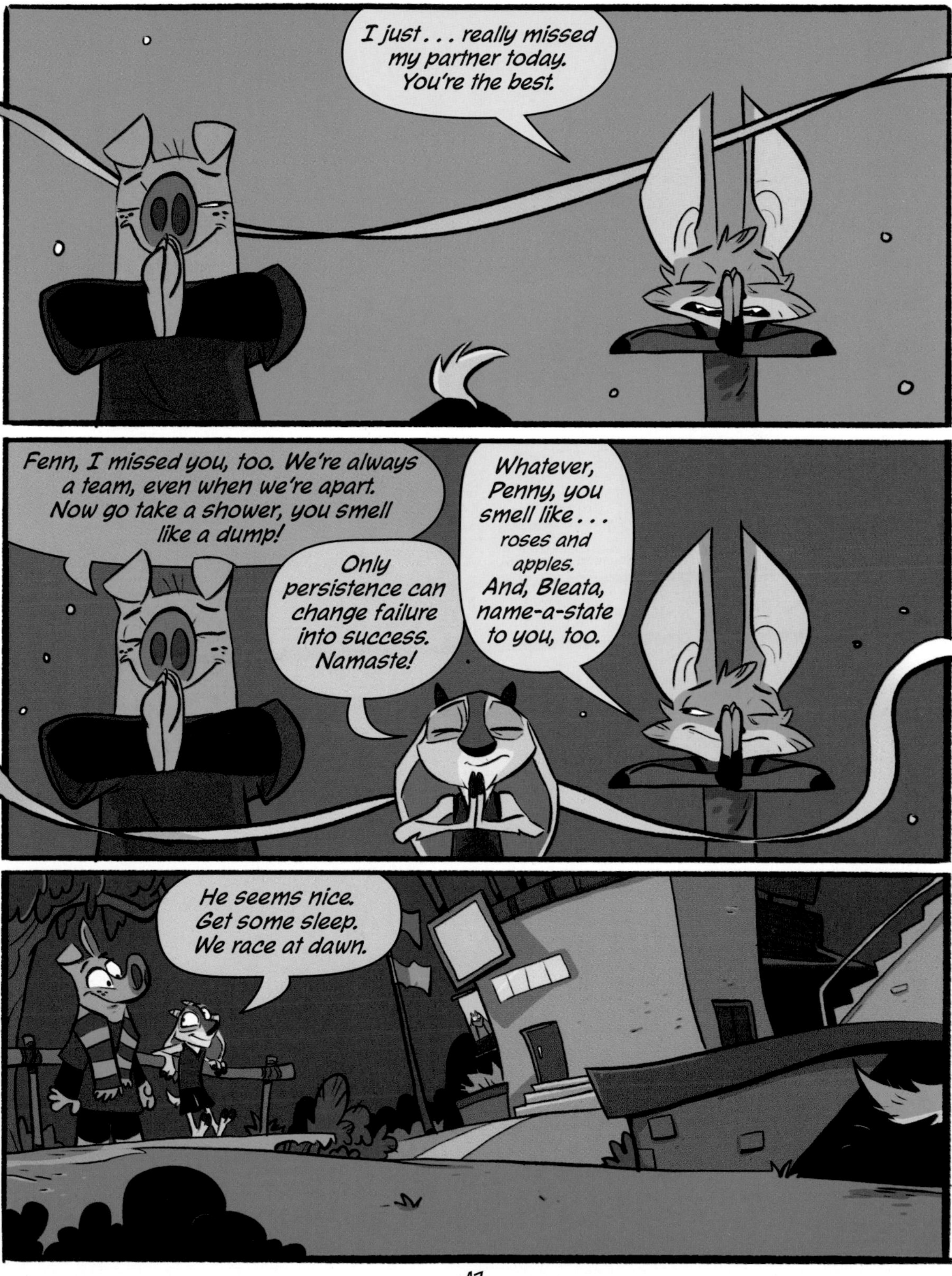
I just . . . really missed my partner today. You're the best.
Fenn, I missed you, too. We're always a team, even when we're apart. Now go take a shower, you smell like a dump!
Only persistence can change failure into success. Namaste!
Whatever, Penny, you smell like . . . roses and apples. And, Bleata, name-a-state to you, too.
He seems nice. Get some sleep. We race at dawn.

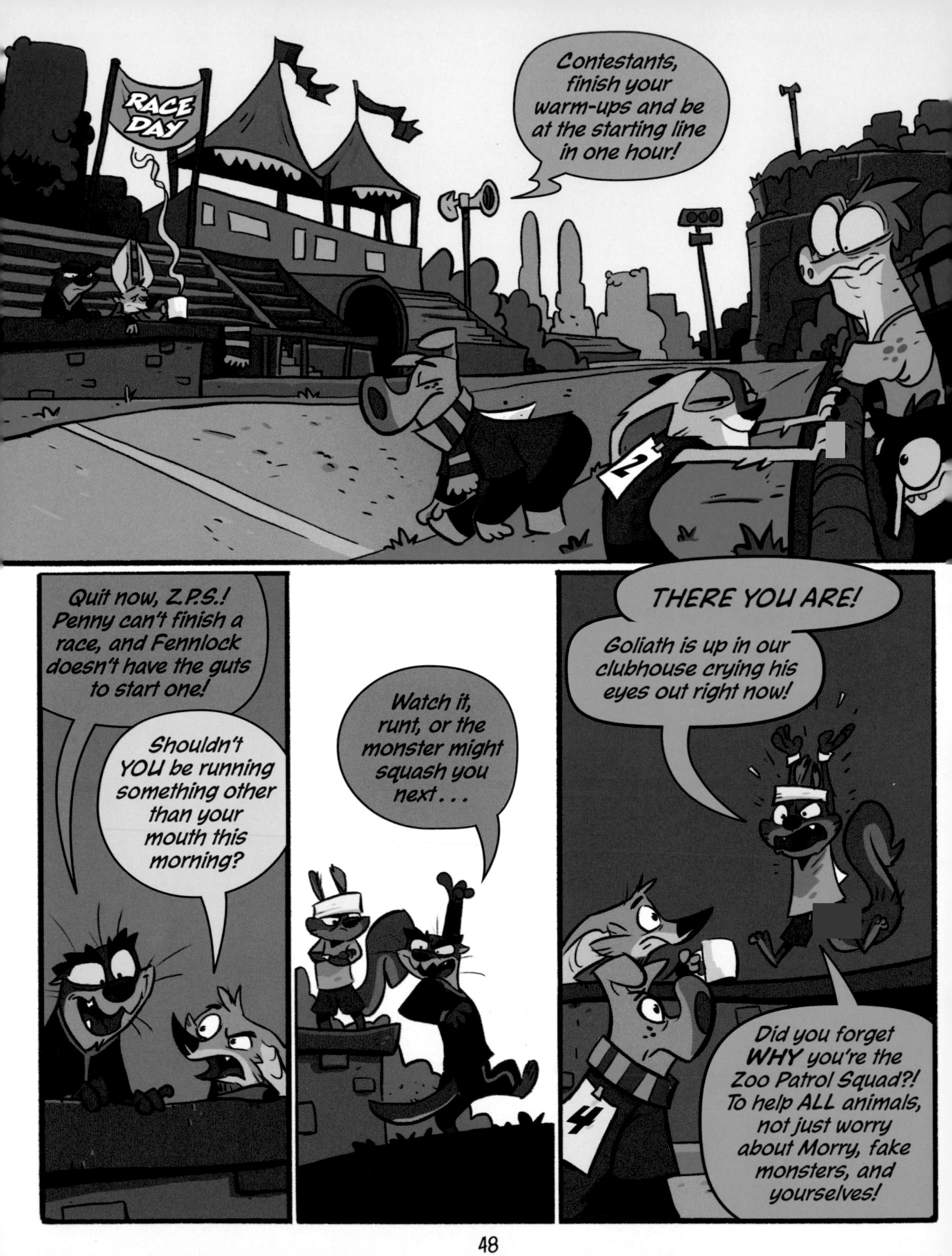
RACE DAY
Contestants, finish your warm-ups and be at the starting line in one hour!
Quit now, Z.P.S.! Penny can't finish a race, and Fennlock doesn't have the guts to start one!
Shouldn't YOU be running something other than your mouth this morning?
Watch it, runt, or the monster might squash you next . . .
THERE YOU ARE!
Goliath is up in our clubhouse crying his eyes out right now!
Did you forget WHY you're the Zoo Patrol Squad?! To help ALL animals, not just worry about Morry, fake monsters, and yourselves!

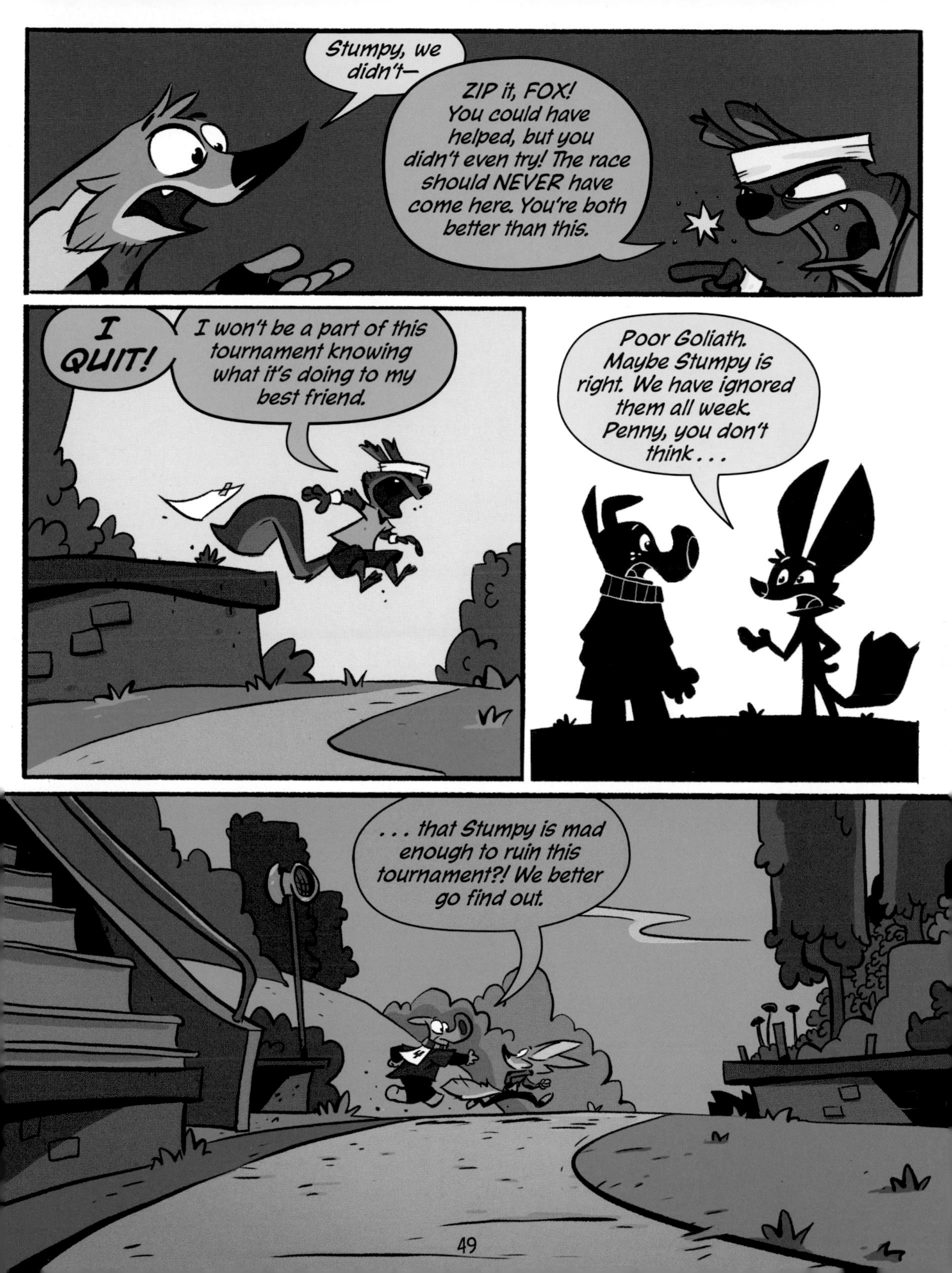
Stumpy, we didn't—
ZIP it, FOX! You could have helped, but you didn't even try! The race should NEVER have come here. You're both better than this.
I QUIT!
I won't be a part of this tournament knowing what it's doing to my best friend.
Poor Goliath. Maybe Stumpy is right. We have ignored them all week. Penny, you don't think . . .
. . . that Stumpy is mad enough to ruin this tournament?! We better go find out.

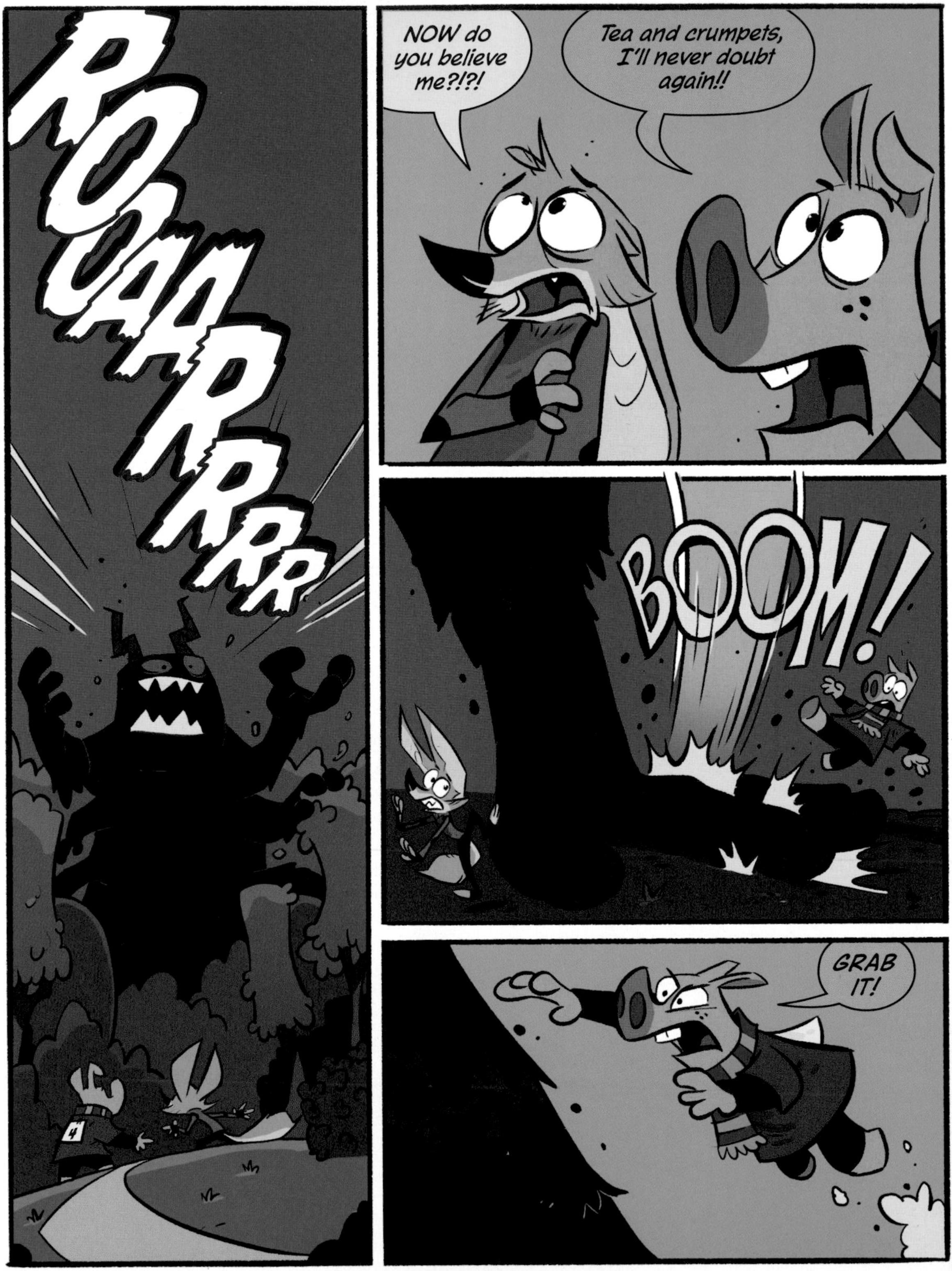
ROOAARRRR
NOW do you believe me?!?!
Tea and crumpets, I'll never doubt again!!
BOOOM!
GRAB IT!

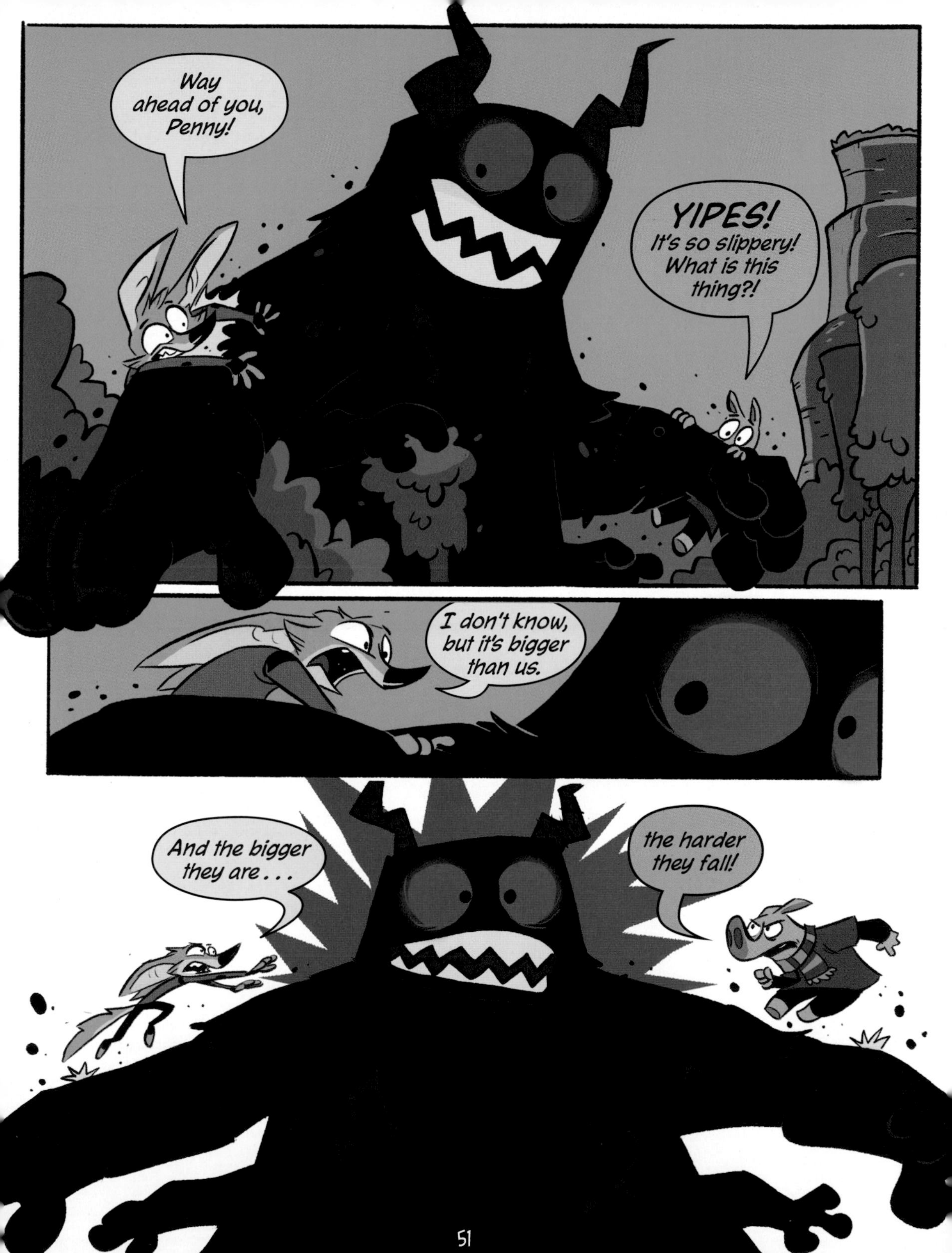
Way ahead of you, Penny!
YIPES! It's so slippery! What is this thing?!
I don't know, but it's bigger than us.
And the bigger they are . . .
the harder they fall!

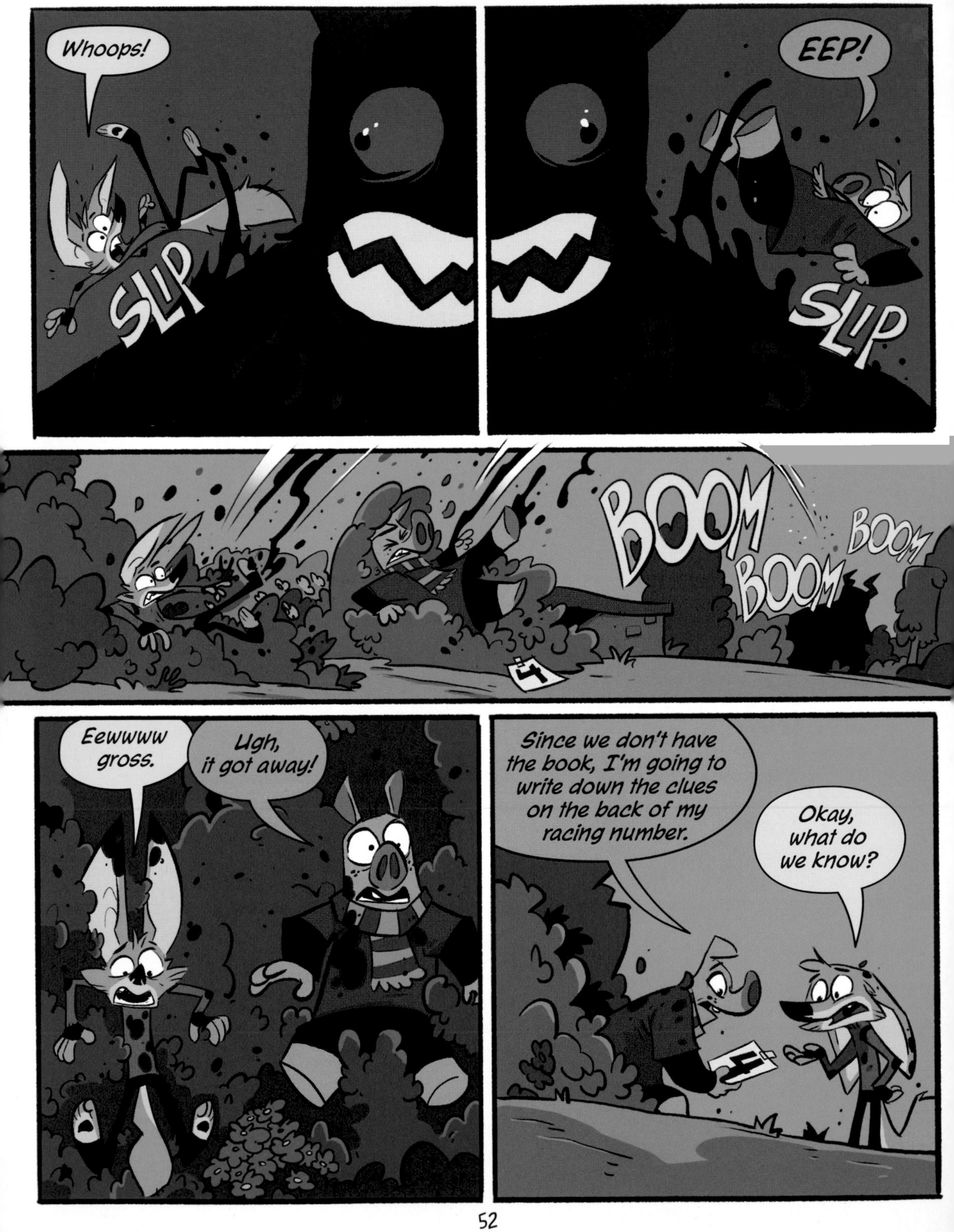

Whoops!
SLIP
EEP!
SLIP
BOOM
BOOM
BOOM
Eewwww gross.
Ugh, it got away!
Since we don't have the book, I'm going to write down the clues on the back of my racing number.
Okay, what do we know?

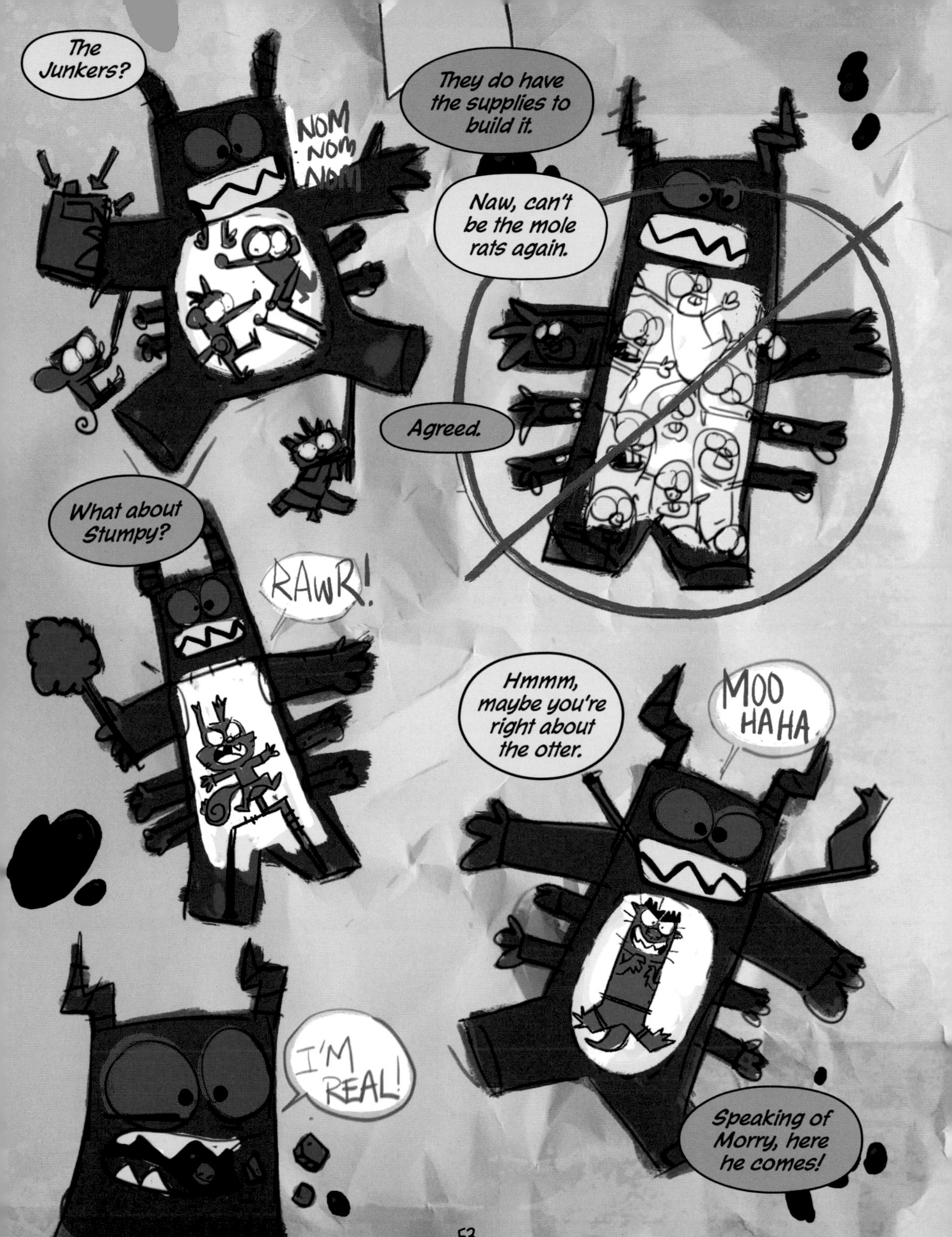
The Junkers?
NOM NOM NOM
They do have the supplies to build it.
Naw, can't be the mole rats again.
Agreed.
What about Stumpy?
RAWR!
Hmmm, maybe you're right about the otter.
MOO HAHA HA
I'M REAL!
Speaking of Morry, here he comes!

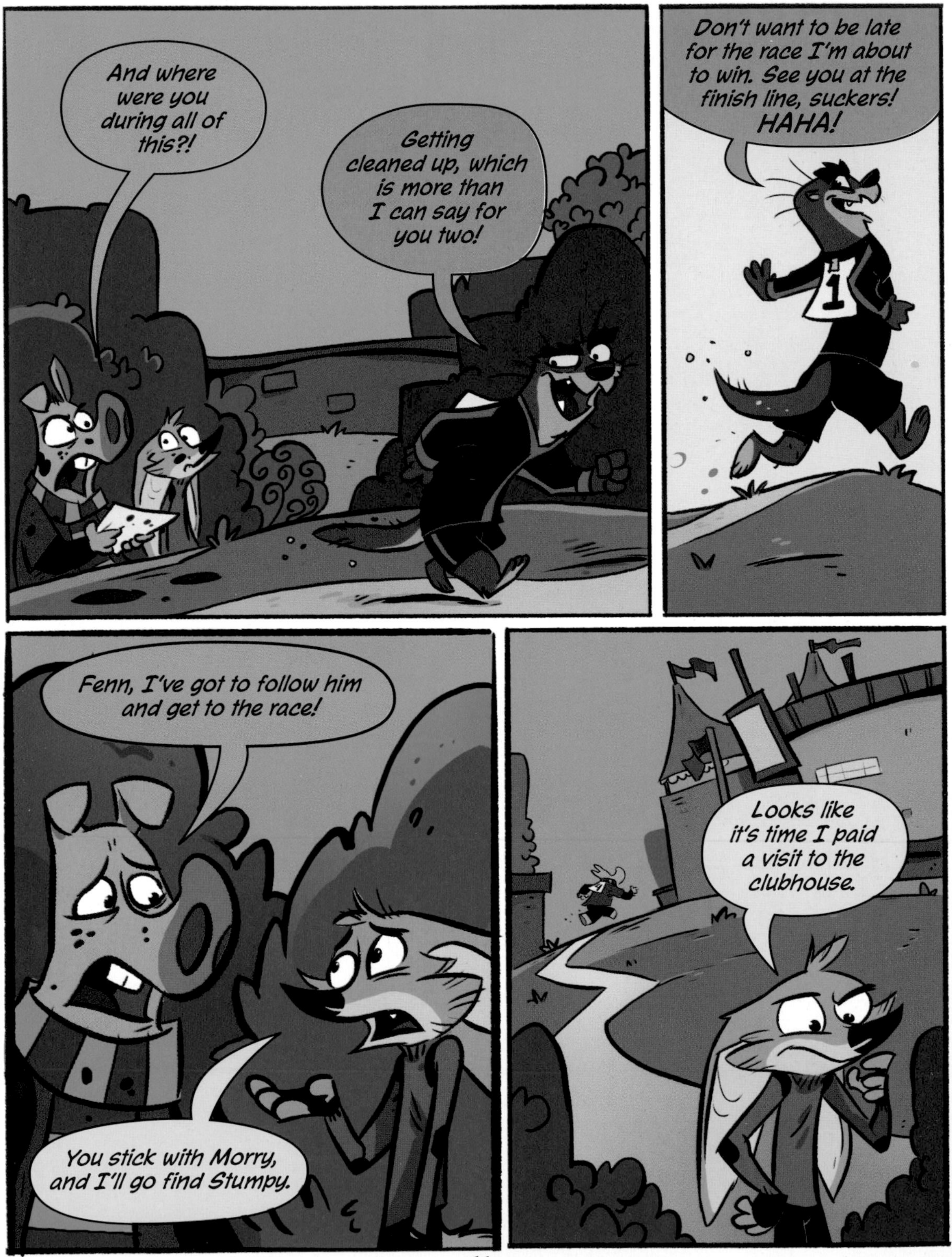
And where were you during all of this?!
Getting cleaned up, which is more than I can say for you two!
Don't want to be late for the race I'm about to win. See you at the finish line, suckers! HAHA!
1
Fenn, I've got to follow him and get to the race!
You stick with Morry, and I'll go find Stumpy.
Looks like it's time I paid a visit to the clubhouse.

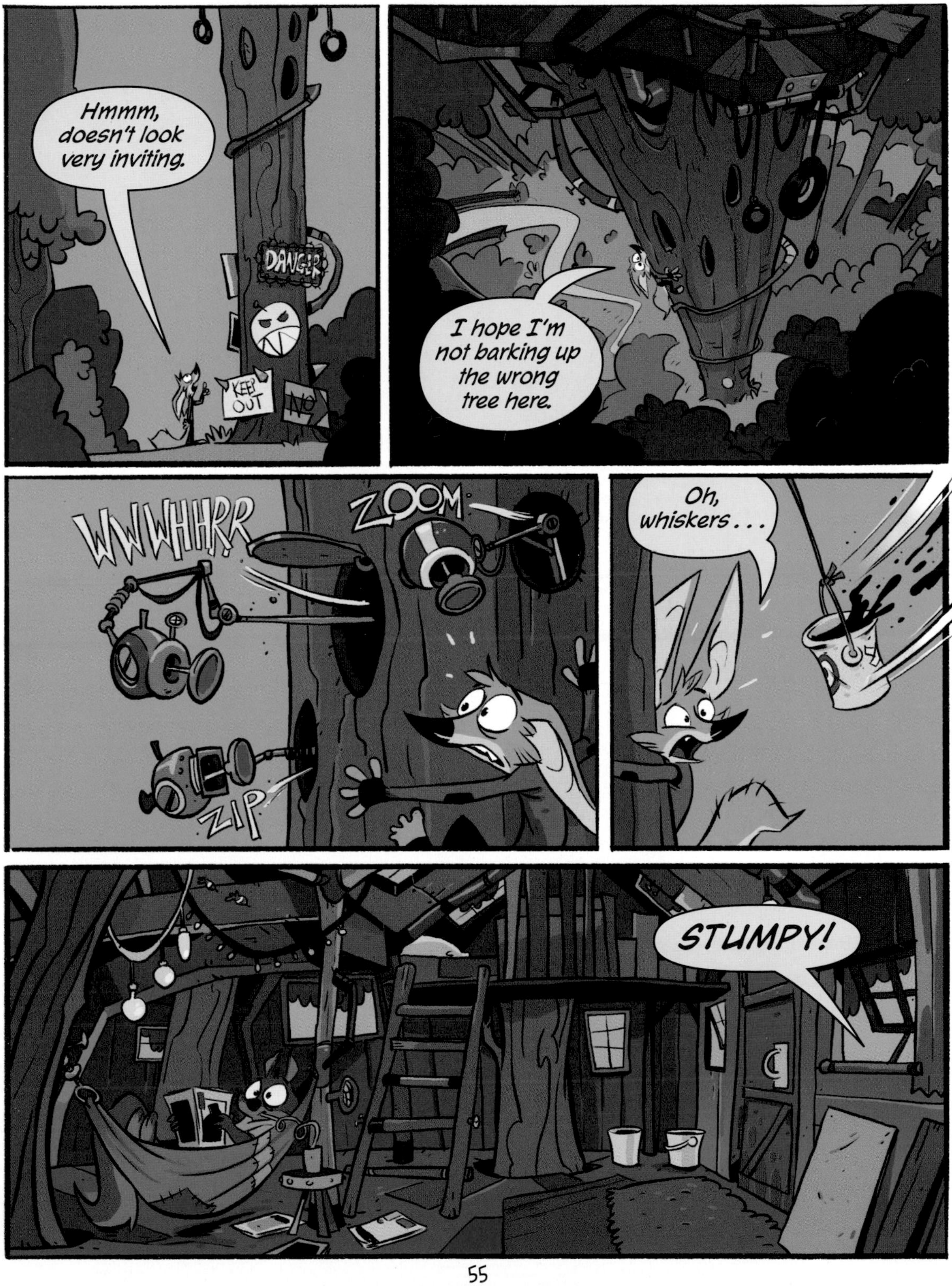

Hmmm, doesn't look very inviting.
DANGER
KEEP OUT
NO
I hope I'm not barking up the wrong tree here.
WWWHHRR
ZOOM
ZIP
Oh, whiskers . . .
STUMPY!

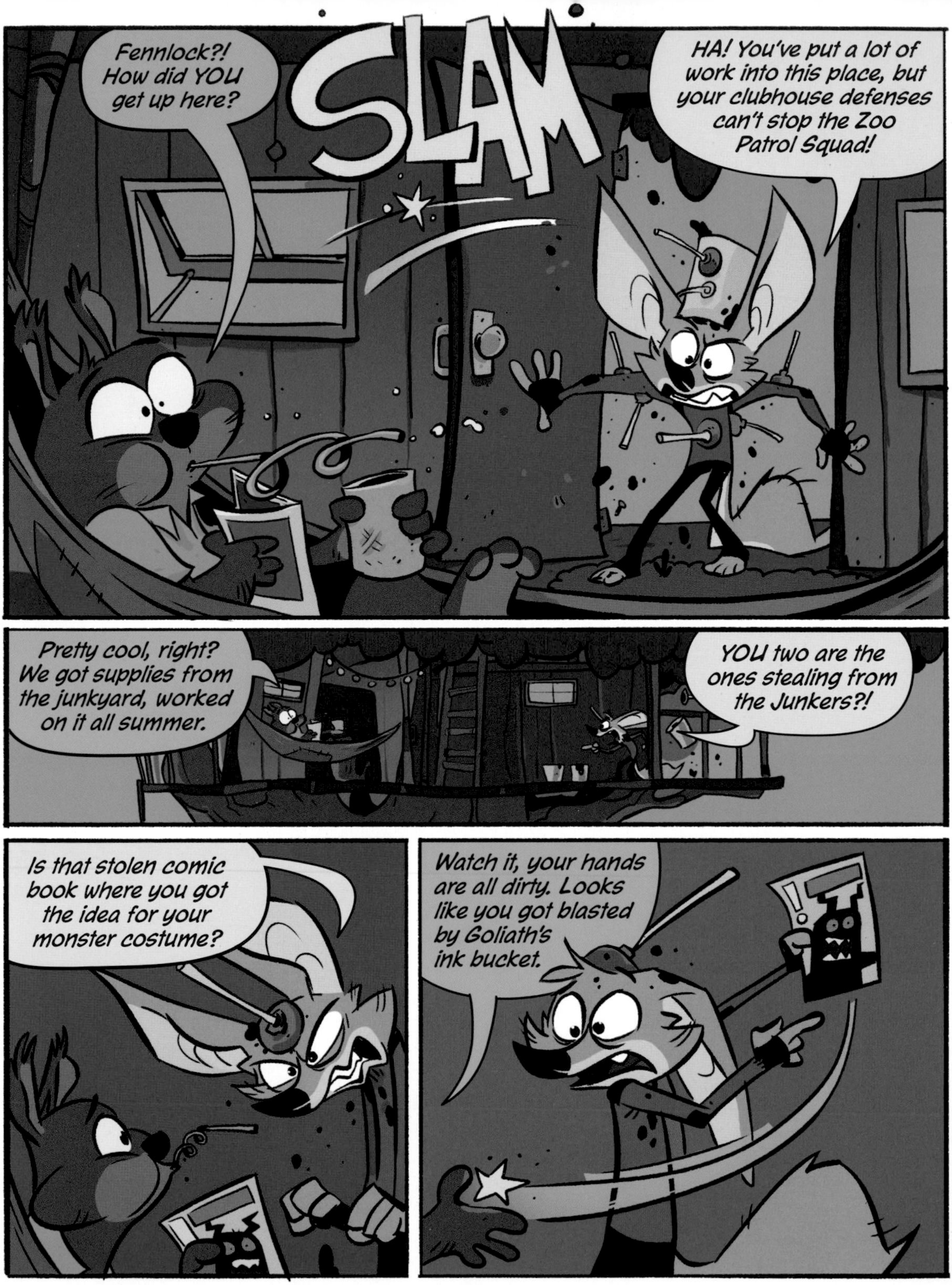
Fennlock?! How did YOU get up here?
SLAM
HA! You've put a lot of work into this place, but your clubhouse defenses can't stop the Zoo Patrol Squad!
Pretty cool, right? We got supplies from the junkyard, worked on it all summer.
YOU two are the ones stealing from the Junkers?!
Is that stolen comic book where you got the idea for your monster costume?
Watch it, your hands are all dirty. Looks like you got blasted by Goliath's ink bucket.

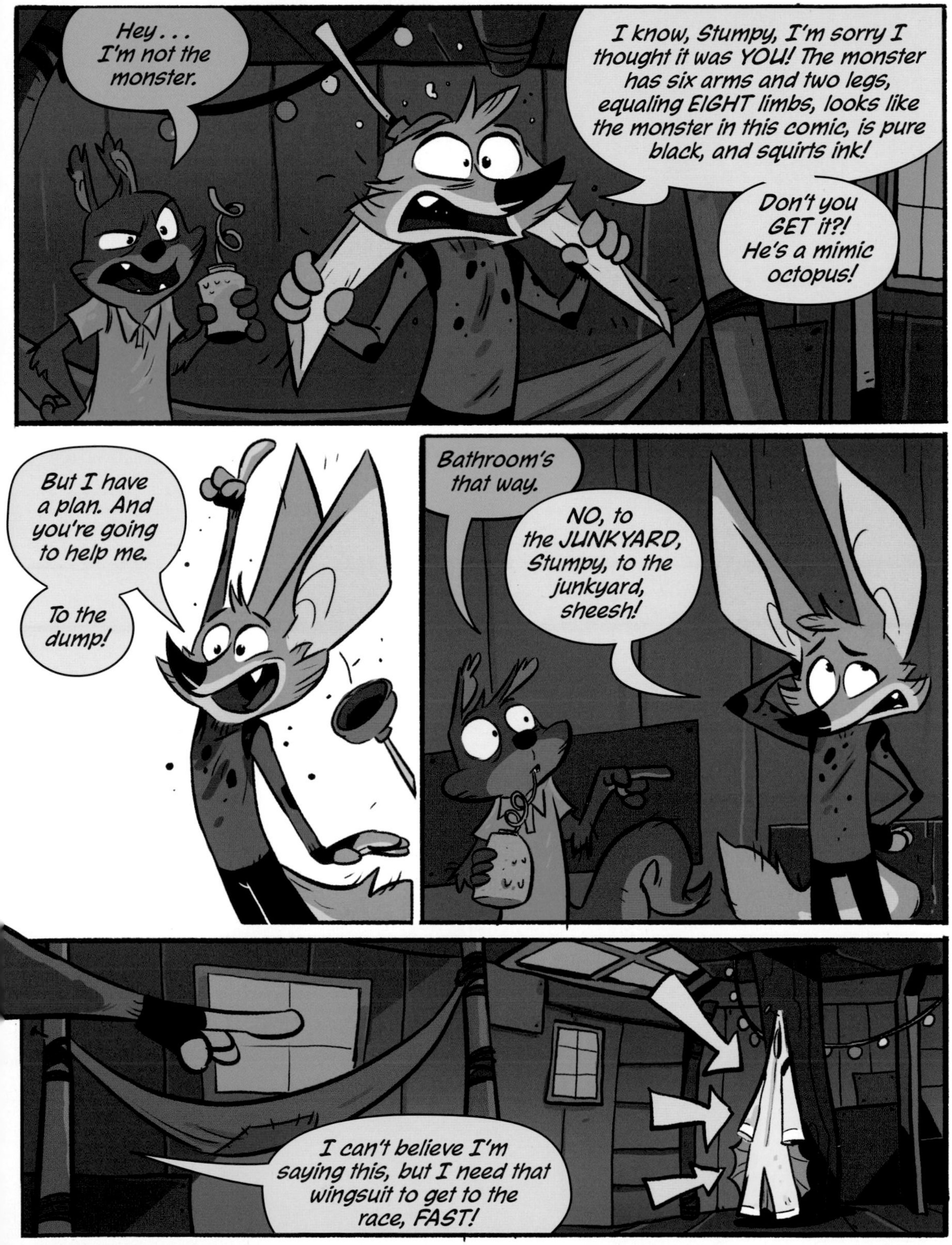
Hey . . . I'm not the monster.
I know, Stumpy, I'm sorry I thought it was YOU! The monster has six arms and two legs, equaling EIGHT limbs, looks like the monster in this comic, is pure black, and squirts ink!
Don't you GET it?! He's a mimic octopus!
But I have a plan. And you're going to help me.
To the dump!
Bathroom's that way.
NO, to the JUNKYARD, Stumpy, to the junkyard, sheesh!
I can't believe I'm saying this, but I need that wingsuit to get to the race, FAST!

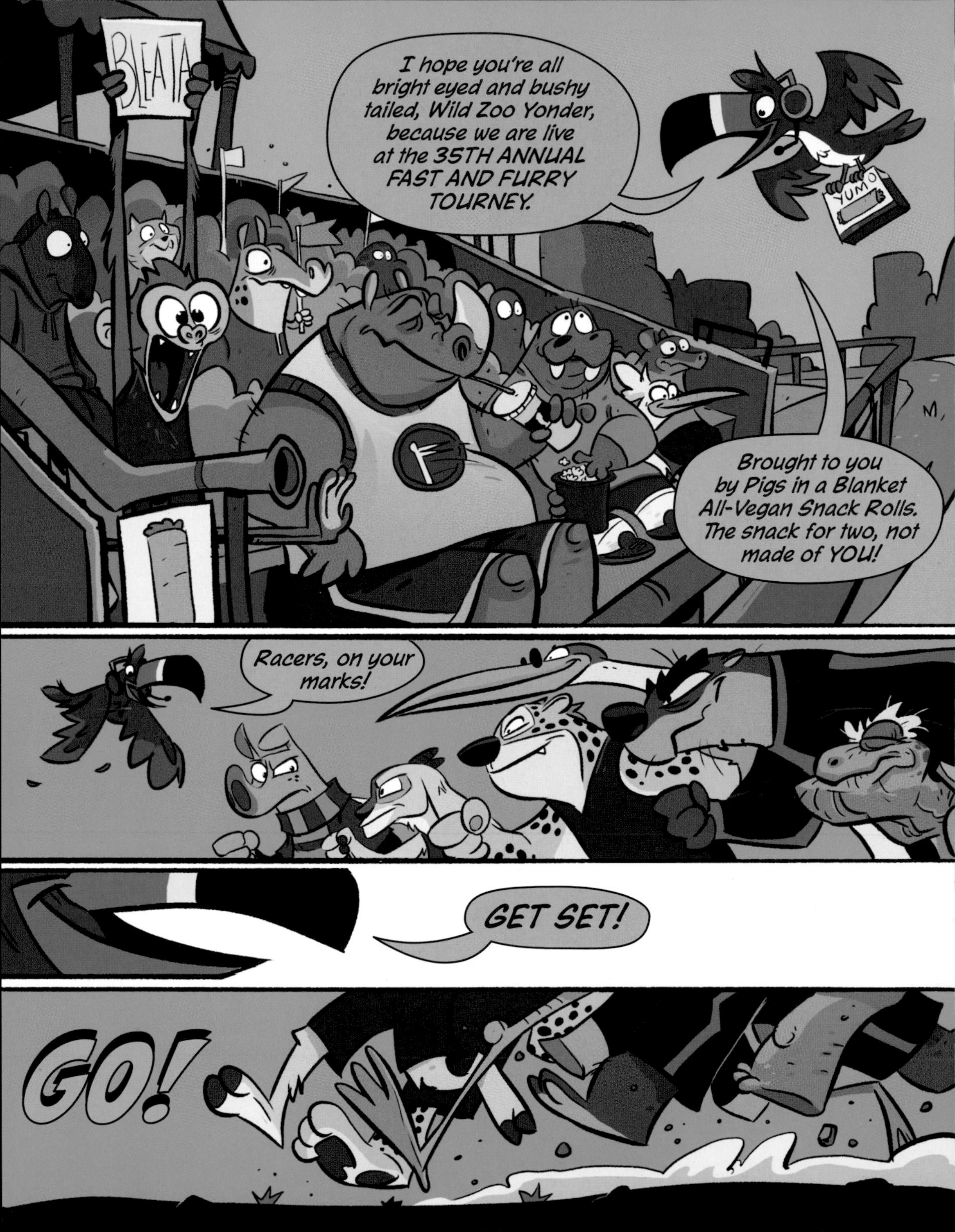
BLEATA
I hope you're all bright eyed and bushy tailed, Wild Zoo Yonder, because we are live at the 35TH ANNUAL FAST AND FURRY TOURNEY.
YUMO
Brought to you by Pigs in a Blanket All-Vegan Snack Rolls. The snack for two, not made of YOU!
Racers, on your marks!
GET SET!
GO!

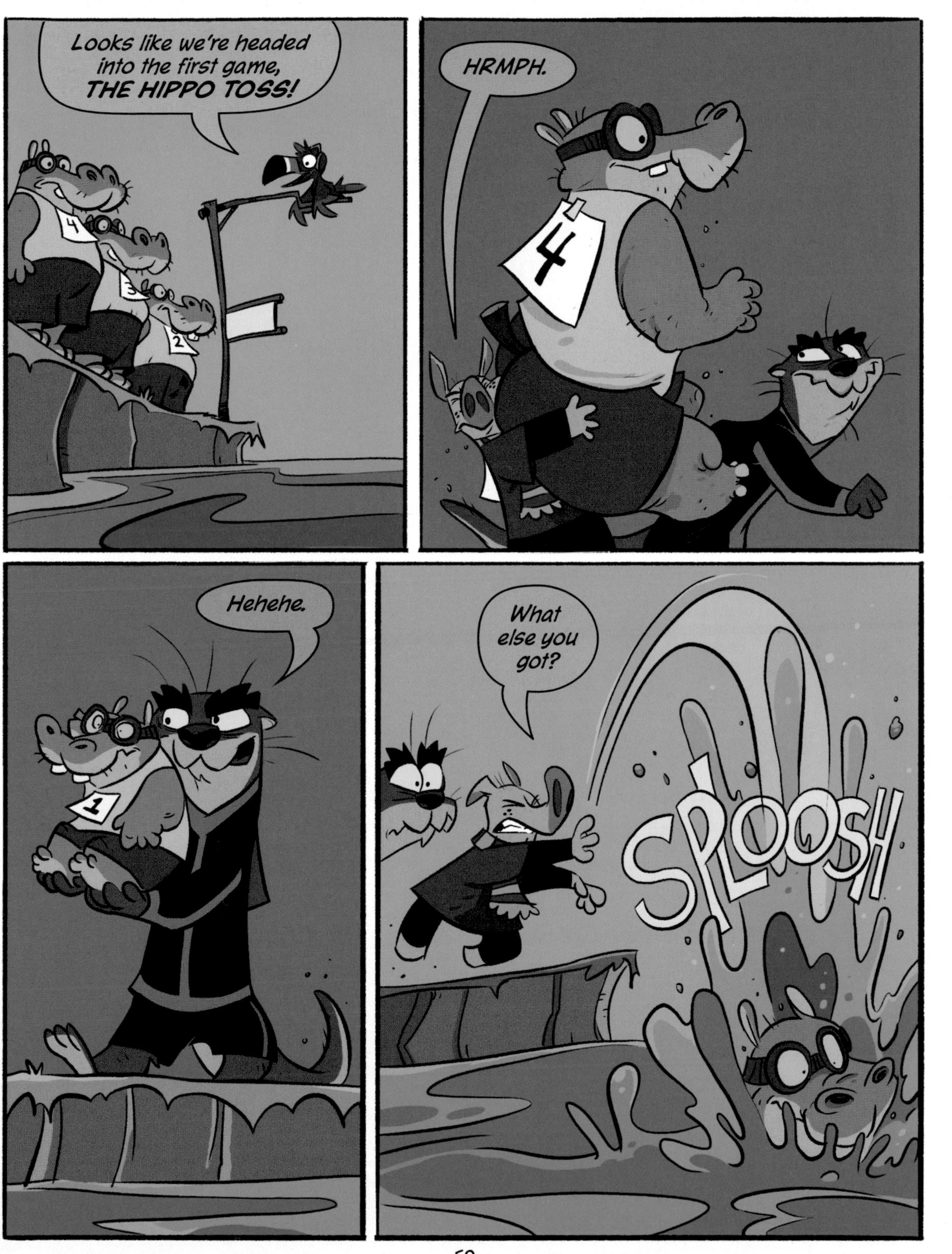

Looks like we're headed into the first game, **THE HIPPO TOSS!**
HRMPH.
Hehehe.
What else you got?
SPLOOSH

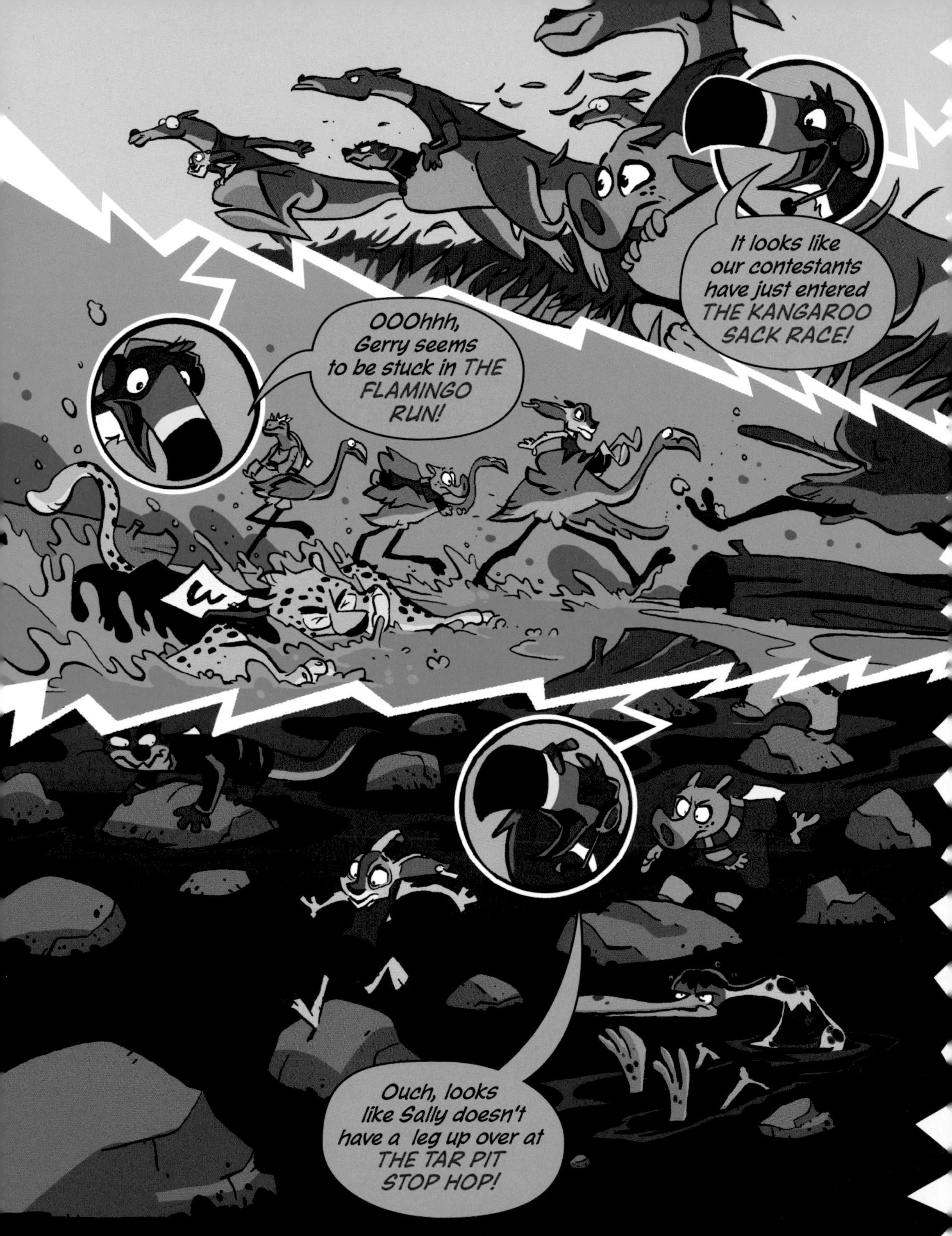
It looks like our contestants have just entered THE KANGAROO SACK RACE!
OOOhhh, Gerry seems to be stuck in THE FLAMINGO RUN!
Ouch, looks like Sally doesn't have a leg up over at THE TAR PIT STOP HOP!

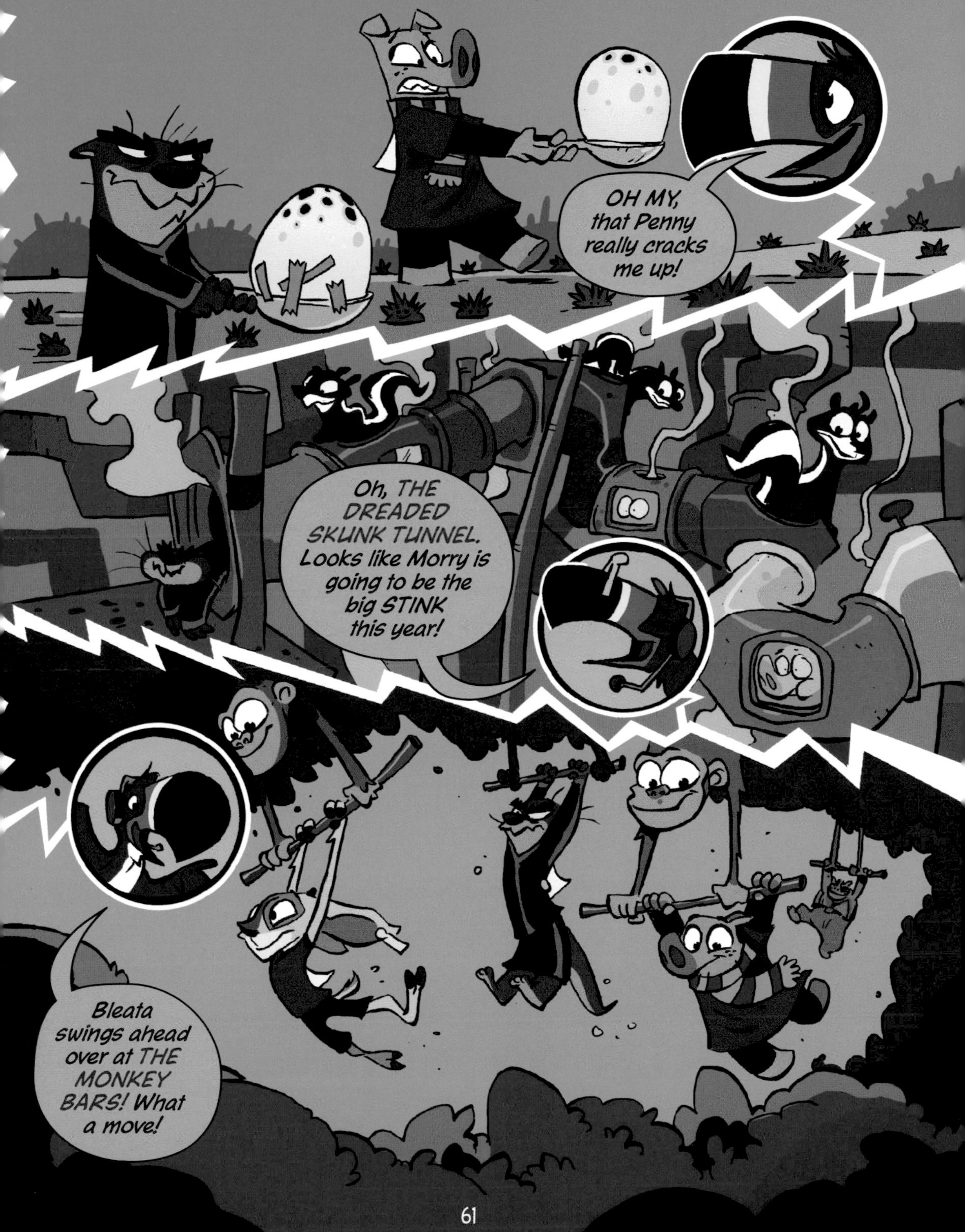
OH MY, that Penny really cracks me up!
Oh, THE DREADED SKUNK TUNNEL. Looks like Morry is going to be the big STINK this year!
Bleata swings ahead over at THE MONKEY BARS! What a move!

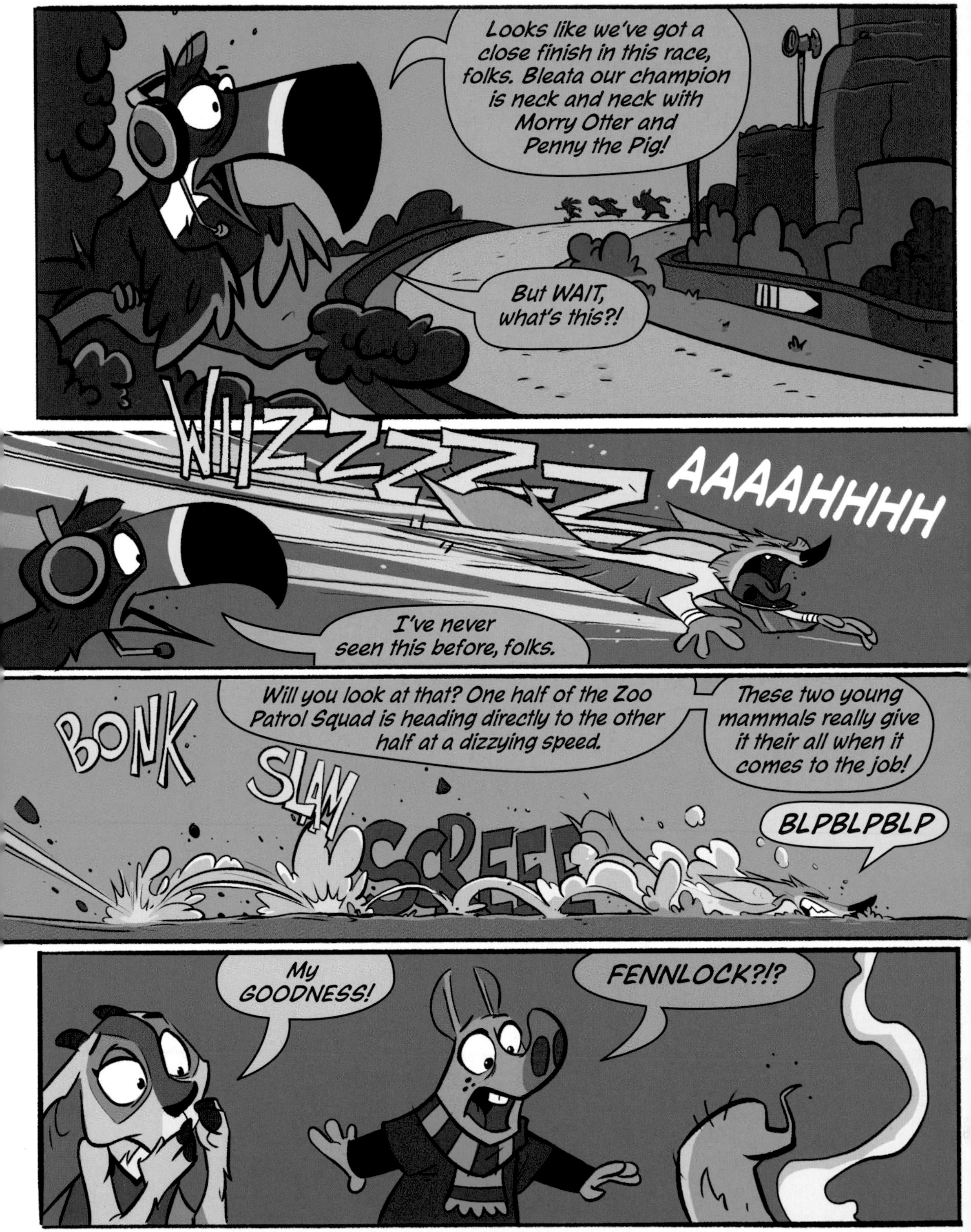
Looks like we've got a close finish in this race, folks. Bleata our champion is neck and neck with Morry Otter and Penny the Pig!
But WAIT, what's this?!
WHIZZZZZ
AAAAHHHH
I've never seen this before, folks.
Will you look at that? One half of the Zoo Patrol Squad is heading directly to the other half at a dizzying speed.
These two young mammals really give it their all when it comes to the job!
BONK
SLAM
SCREEE
BLPBLPBLP
My GOODNESS!
FENNLOCK?!?

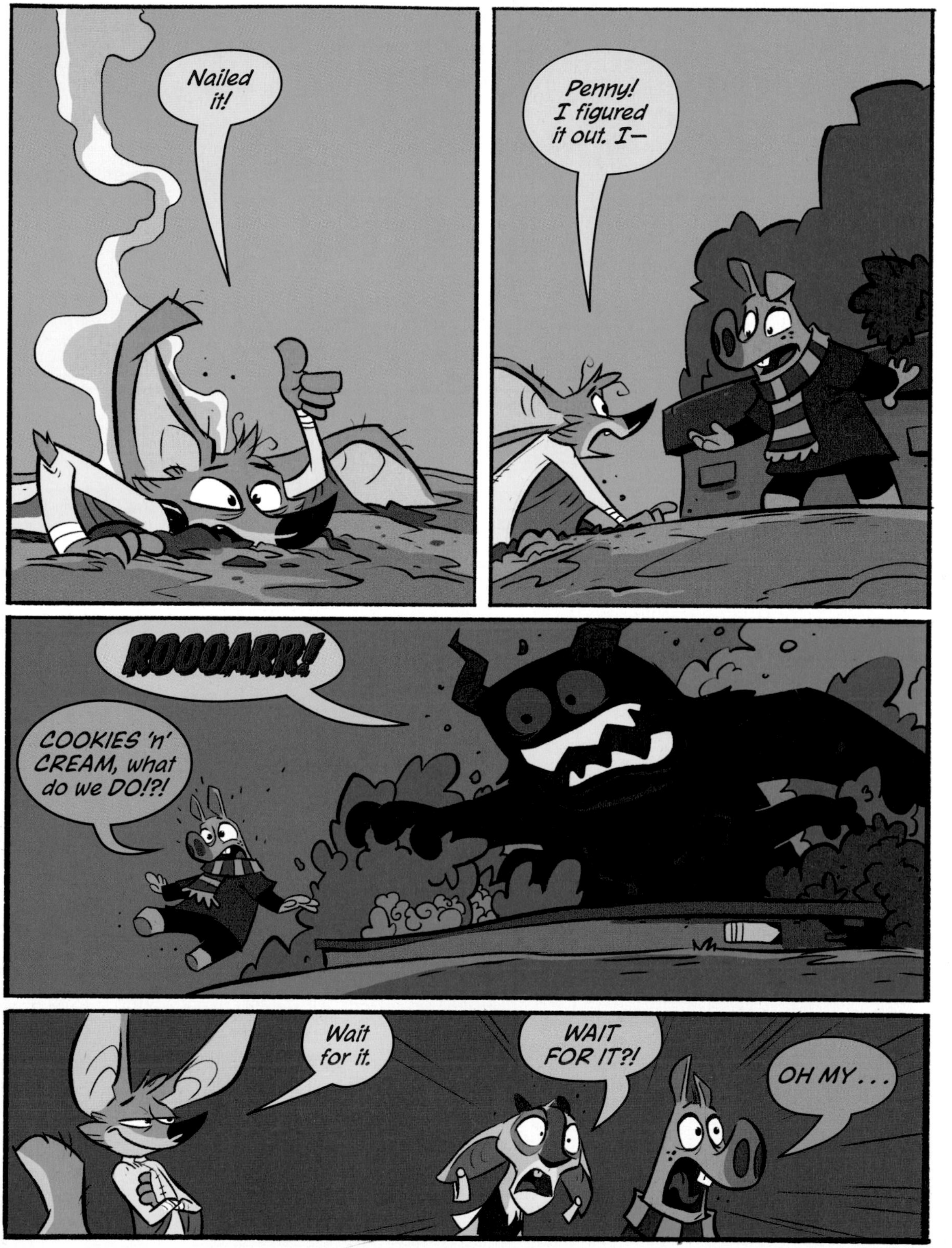
Nailed it!
Penny! I figured it out. I—
ROOOARR!
COOKIES 'n' CREAM, what do we DO!?!
Wait for it.
WAIT FOR IT?!
OH MY . . .

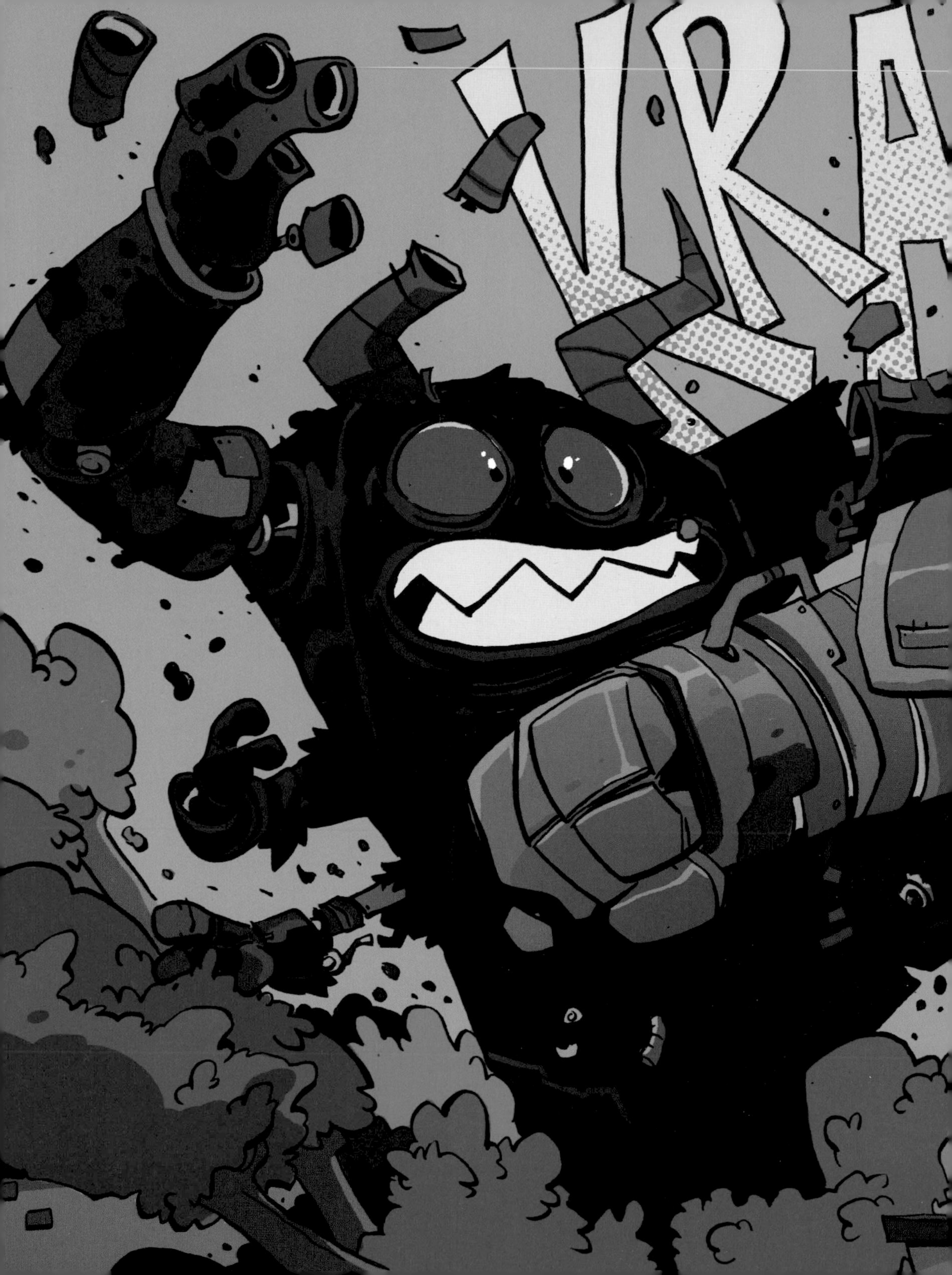
VRA

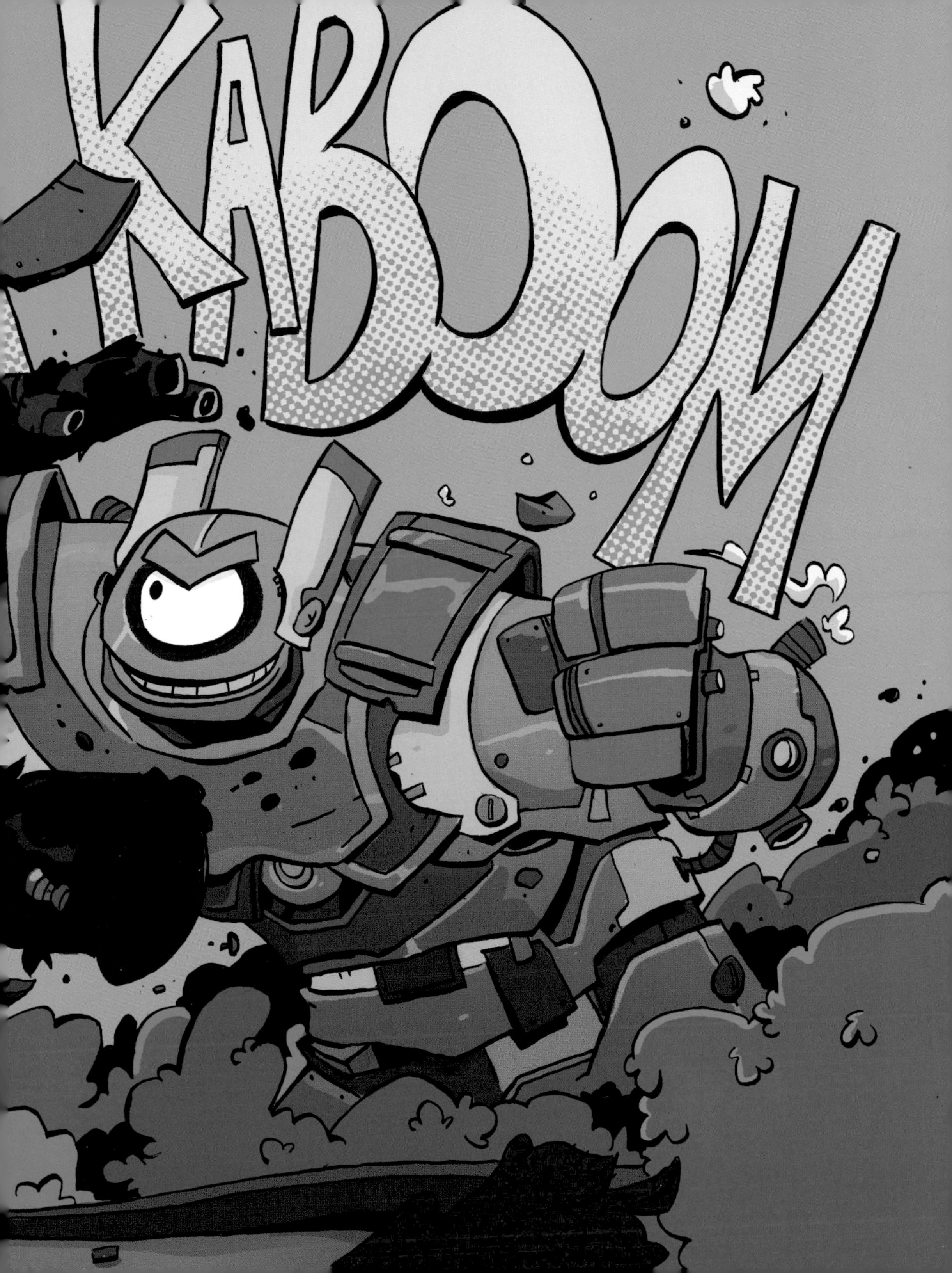
KABOOM

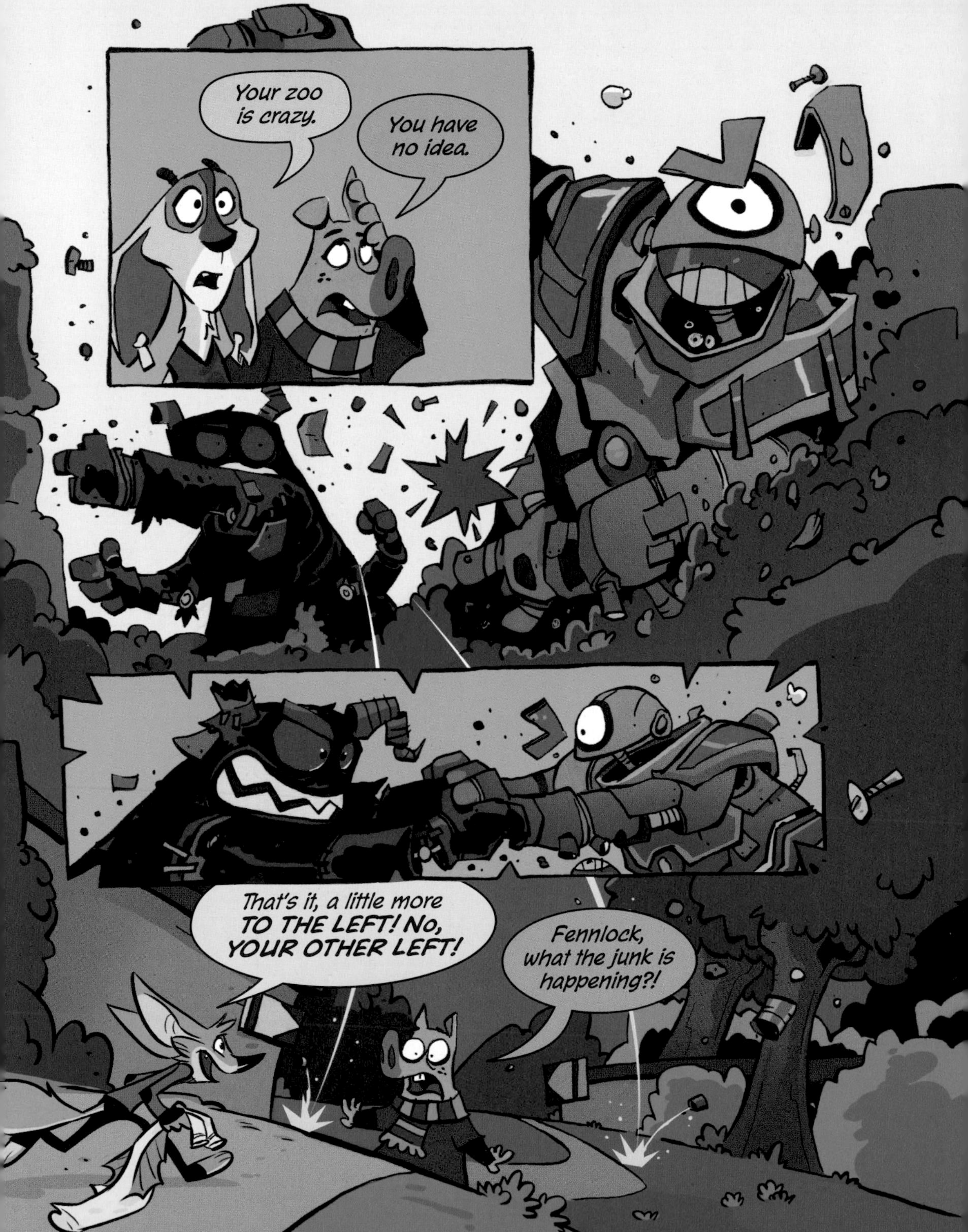
Your zoo is crazy.
You have no idea.
That's it, a little more TO THE LEFT! No, YOUR OTHER LEFT!
Fennlock, what the junk is happening?!

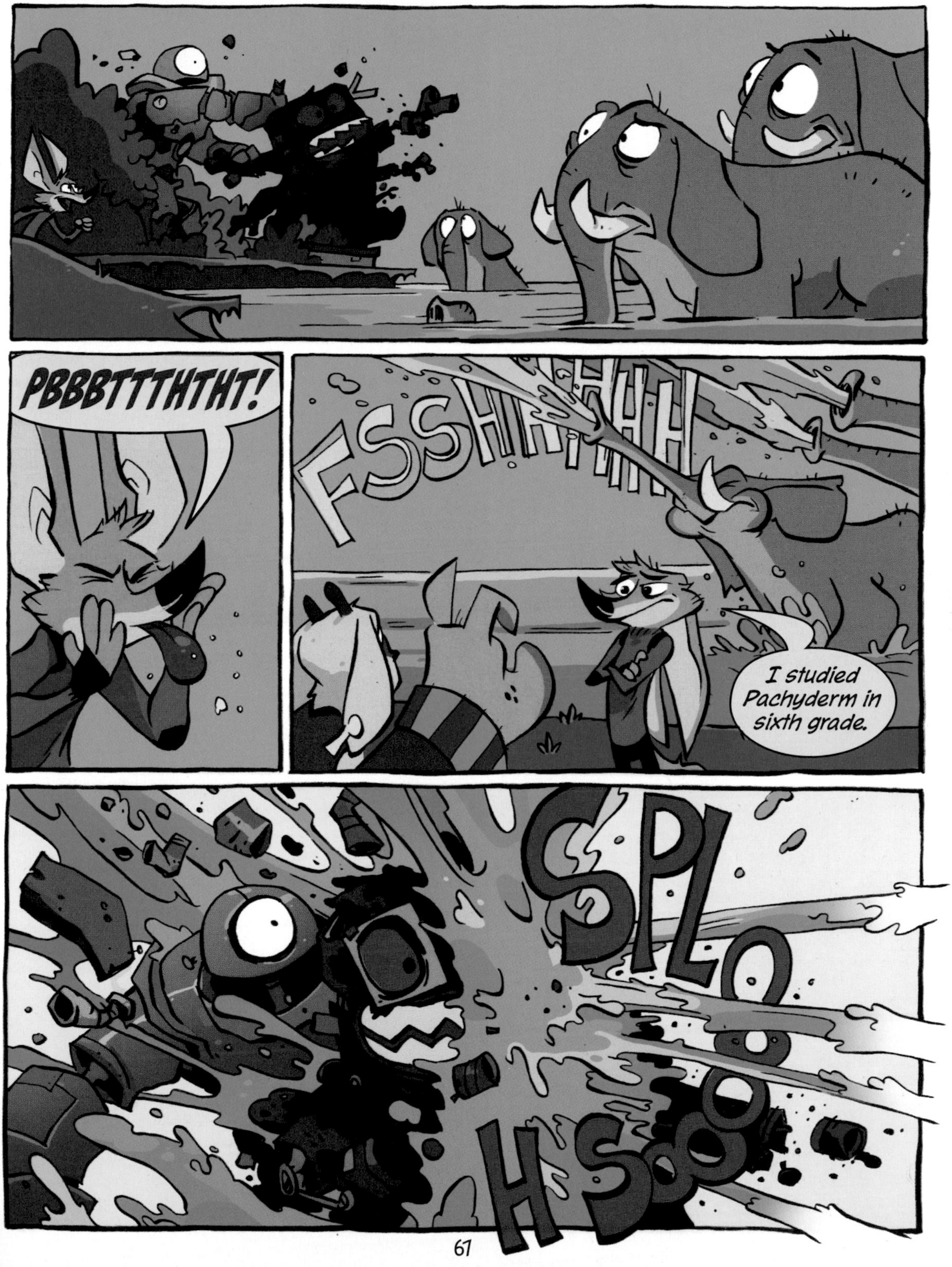
PBBBTTTHTHT!
FSSHHHHHH
I studied Pachyderm in sixth grade.
SPLOOSH

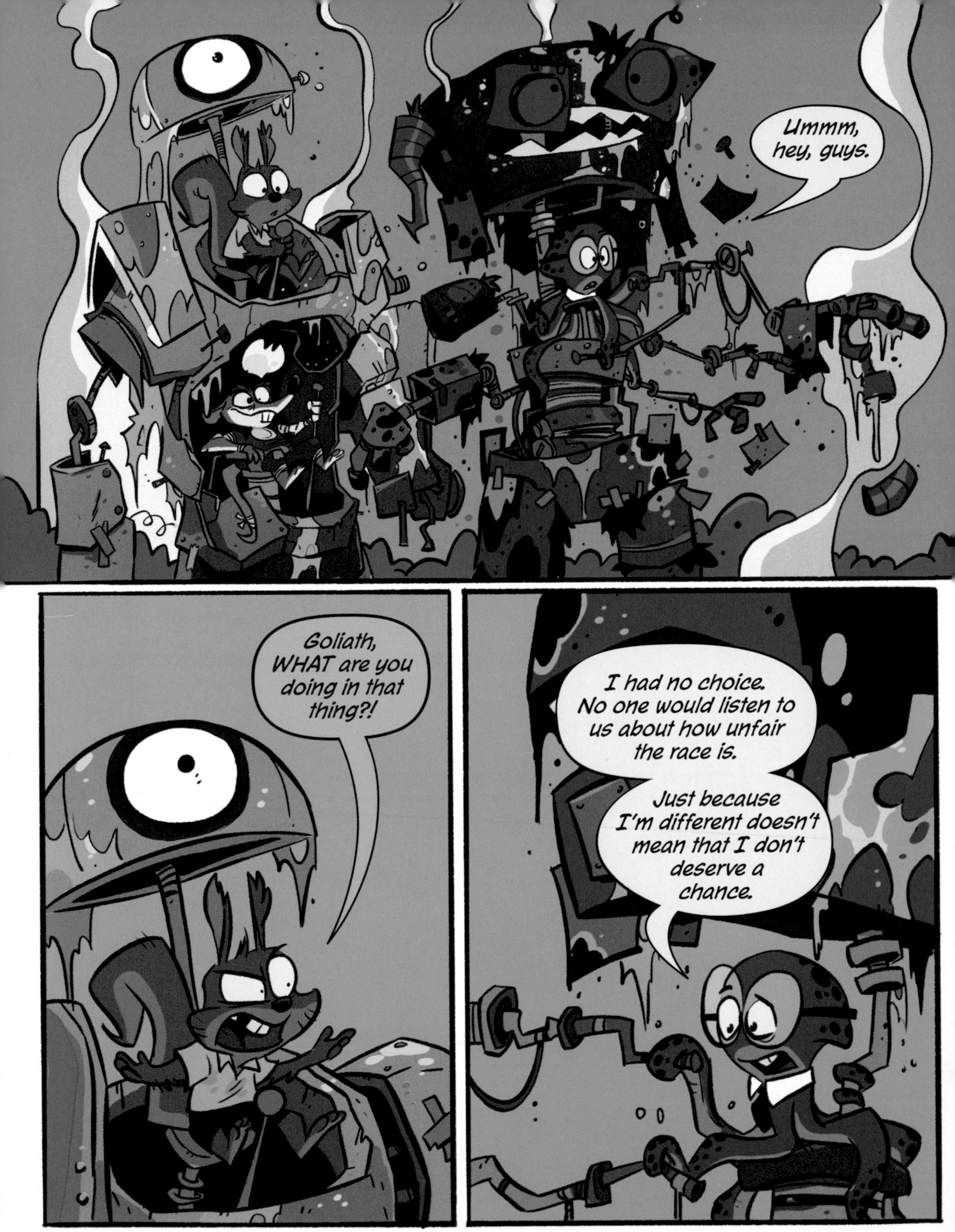
Ummm, hey, guys.
Goliath, WHAT are you doing in that thing?!
I had no choice. No one would listen to us about how unfair the race is.
Just because I'm different doesn't mean that I don't deserve a chance.

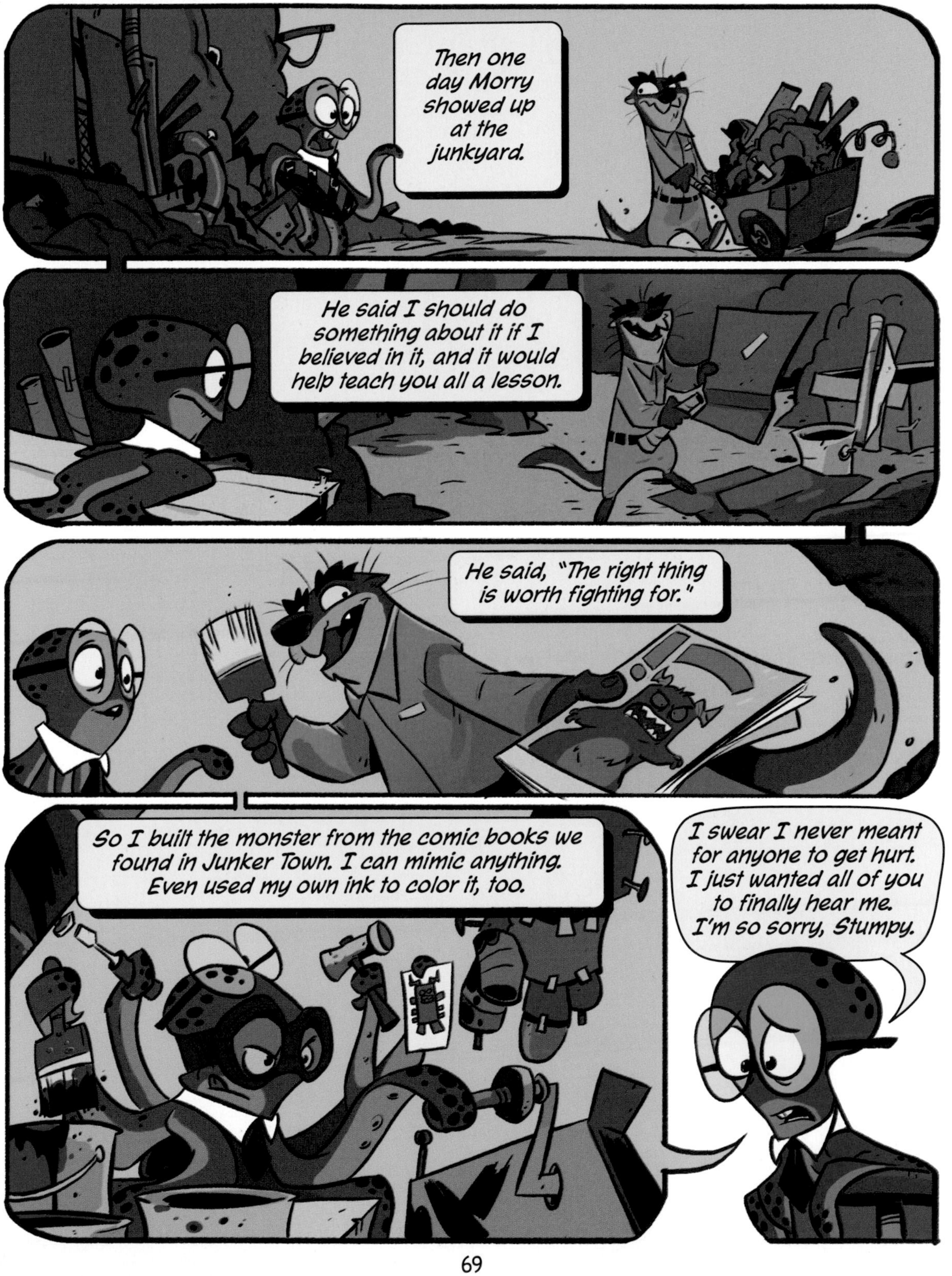

Then one day Morry showed up at the junkyard.
He said I should do something about it if I believed in it, and it would help teach you all a lesson.
He said, "The right thing is worth fighting for."
So I built the monster from the comic books we found in Junker Town. I can mimic anything. Even used my own ink to color it, too.
I swear I never meant for anyone to get hurt. I just wanted all of you to finally hear me. I'm so sorry, Stumpy.

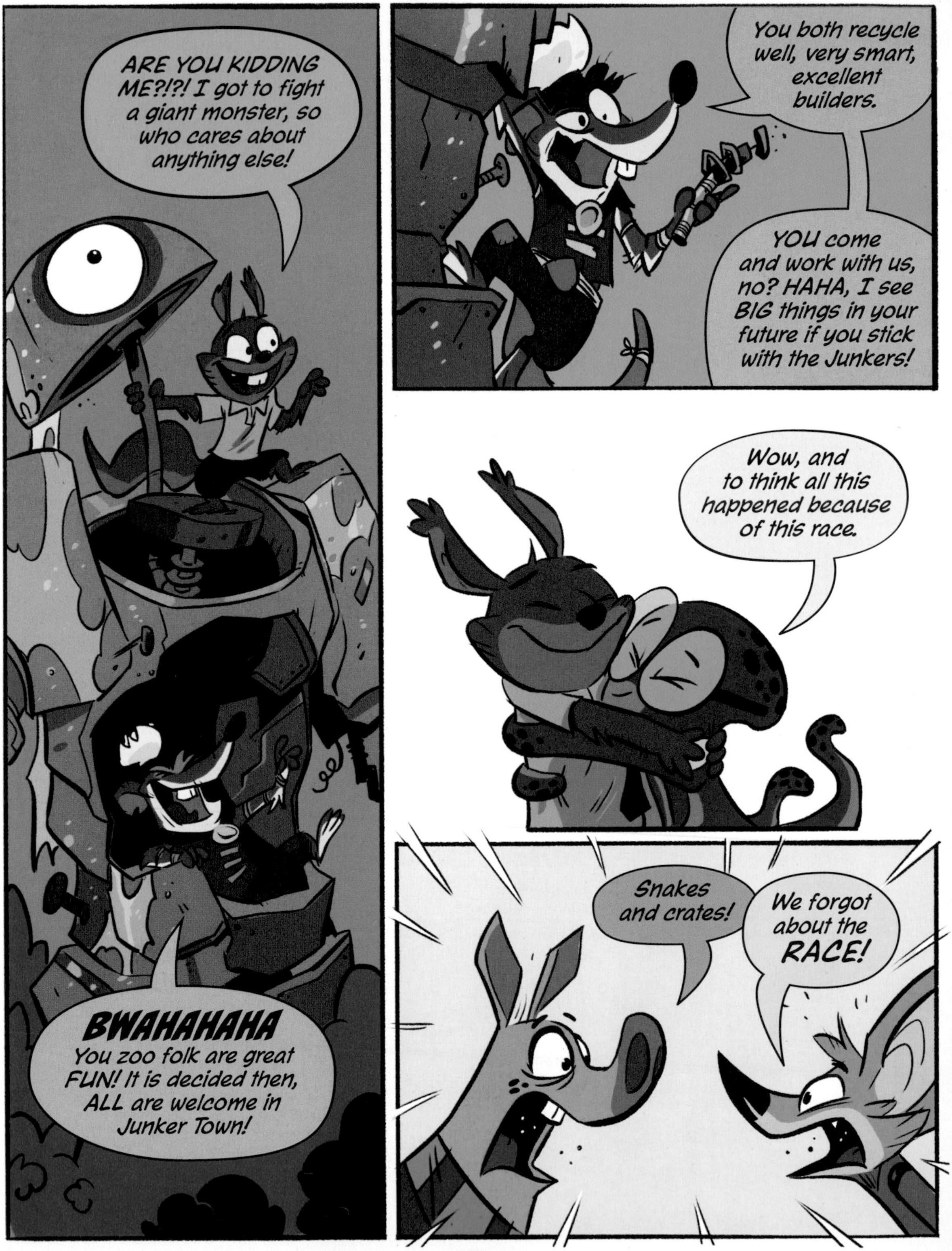
ARE YOU KIDDING ME?!?! I got to fight a giant monster, so who cares about anything else!
BWAHAHAHA You zoo folk are great FUN! It is decided then, ALL are welcome in Junker Town!
You both recycle well, very smart, excellent builders.
YOU come and work with us, no? HAHA, I see BIG things in your future if you stick with the Junkers!
Wow, and to think all this happened because of this race.
Snakes and crates!
We forgot about the RACE!

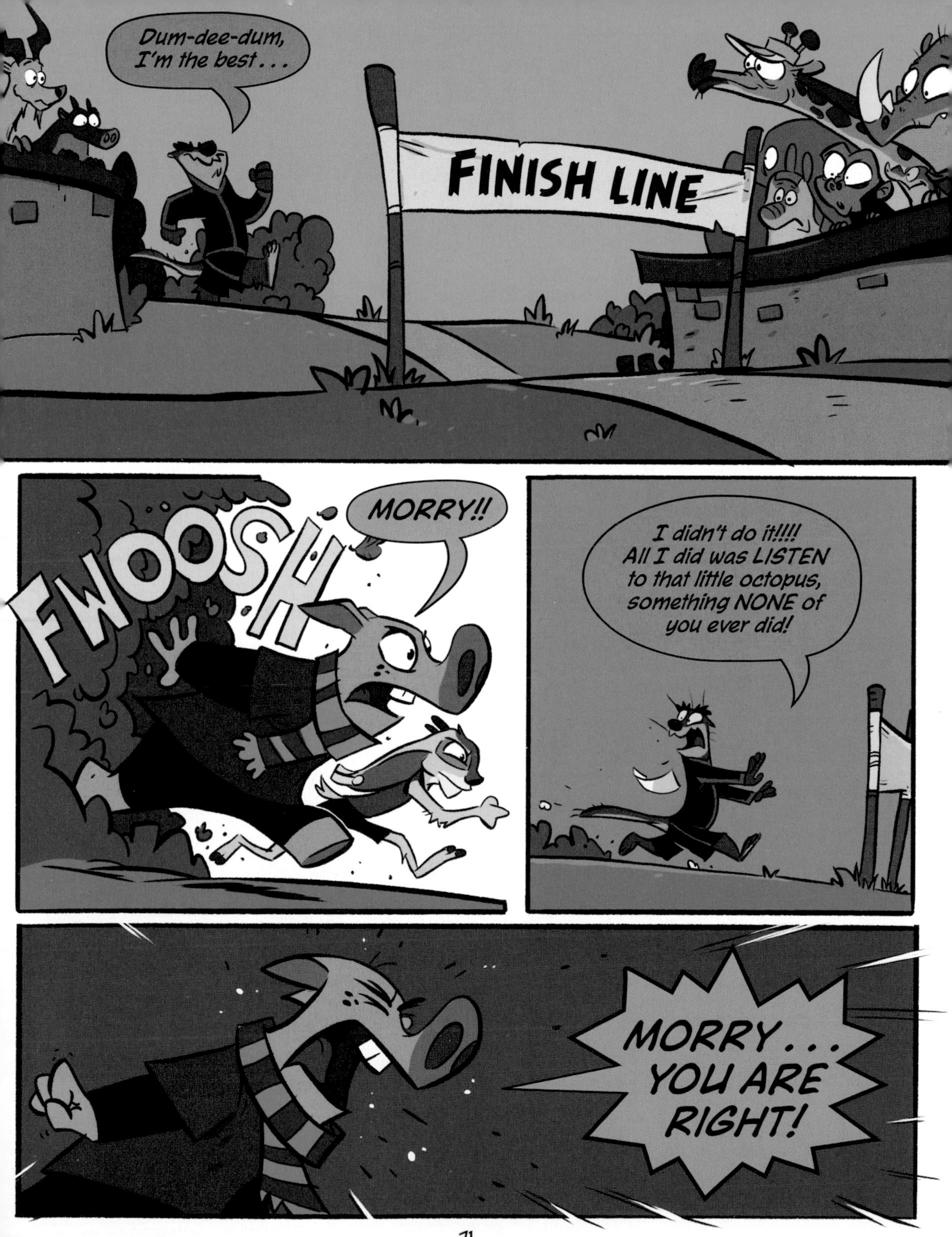
Dum-dee-dum, I'm the best . . .
FINISH LINE
FWOOSH
MORRY!!
I didn't do it!!!! All I did was LISTEN to that little octopus, something NONE of you ever did!
MORRY . . . YOU ARE RIGHT!

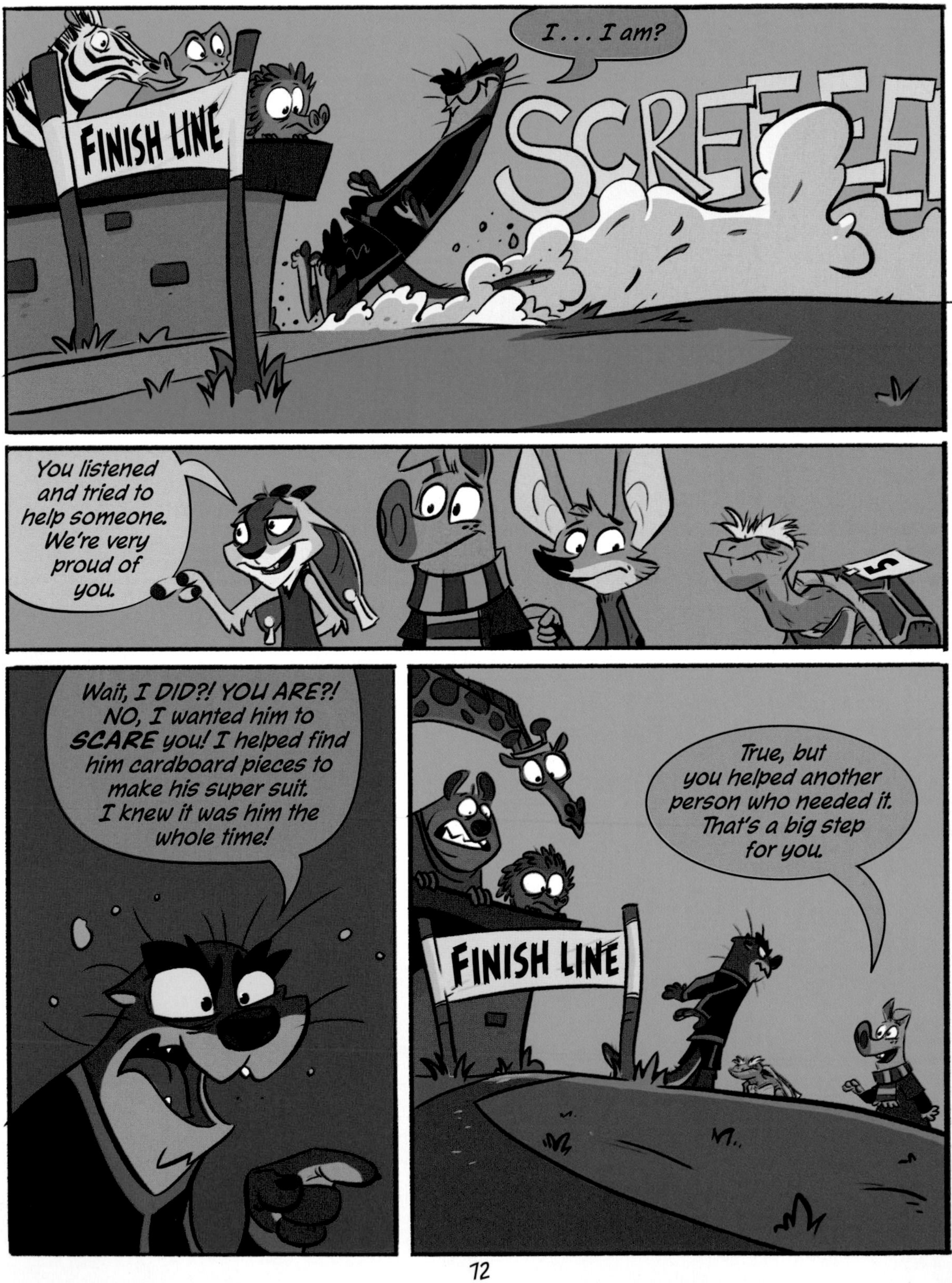
FINISH LINE
I . . . I am?
SCREEEEE
You listened and tried to help someone. We're very proud of you.
5
Wait, I DID?! YOU ARE?! NO, I wanted him to SCARE you! I helped find him cardboard pieces to make his super suit. I knew it was him the whole time!
FINISH LINE
True, but you helped another person who needed it. That's a big step for you.

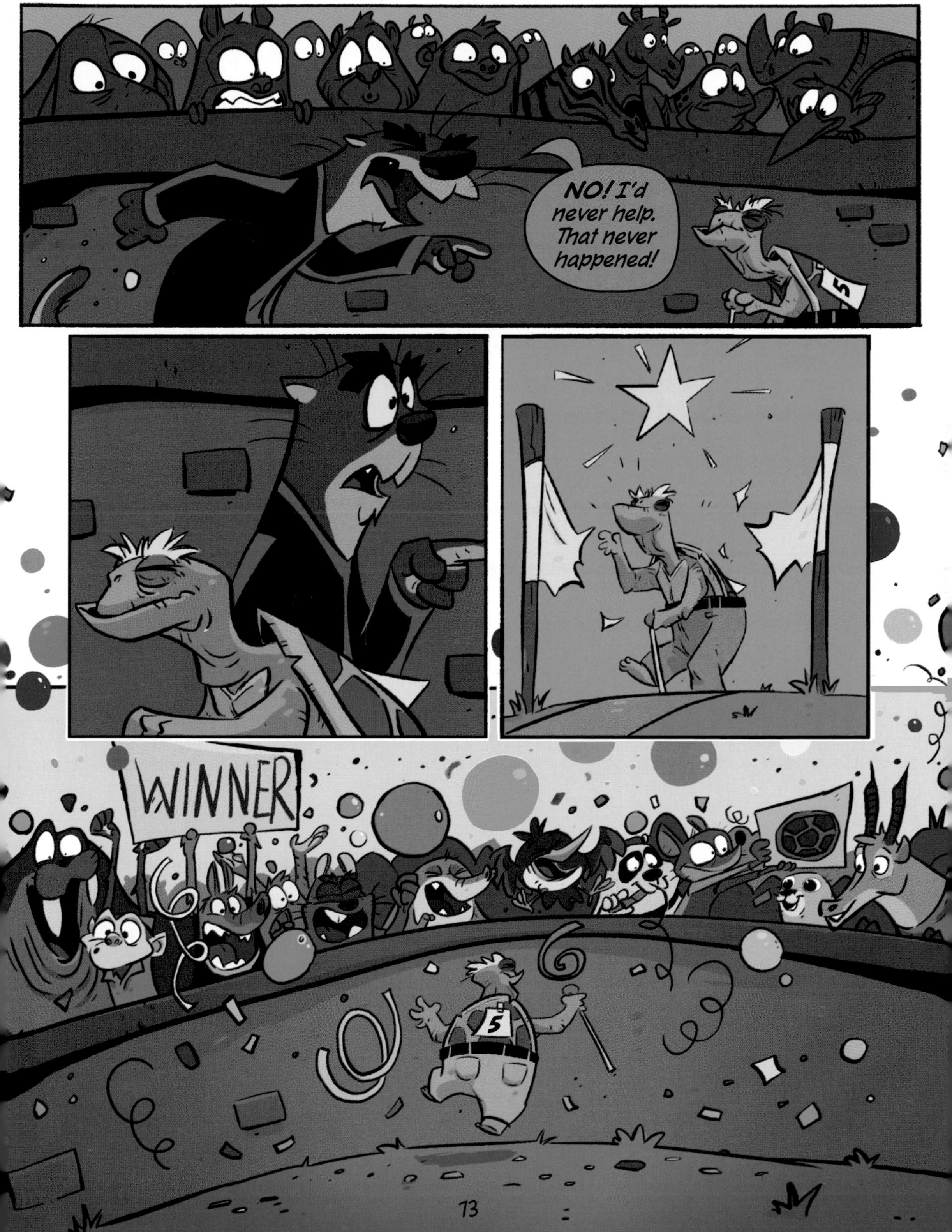
NO! I'd never help. That never happened!
WINNER

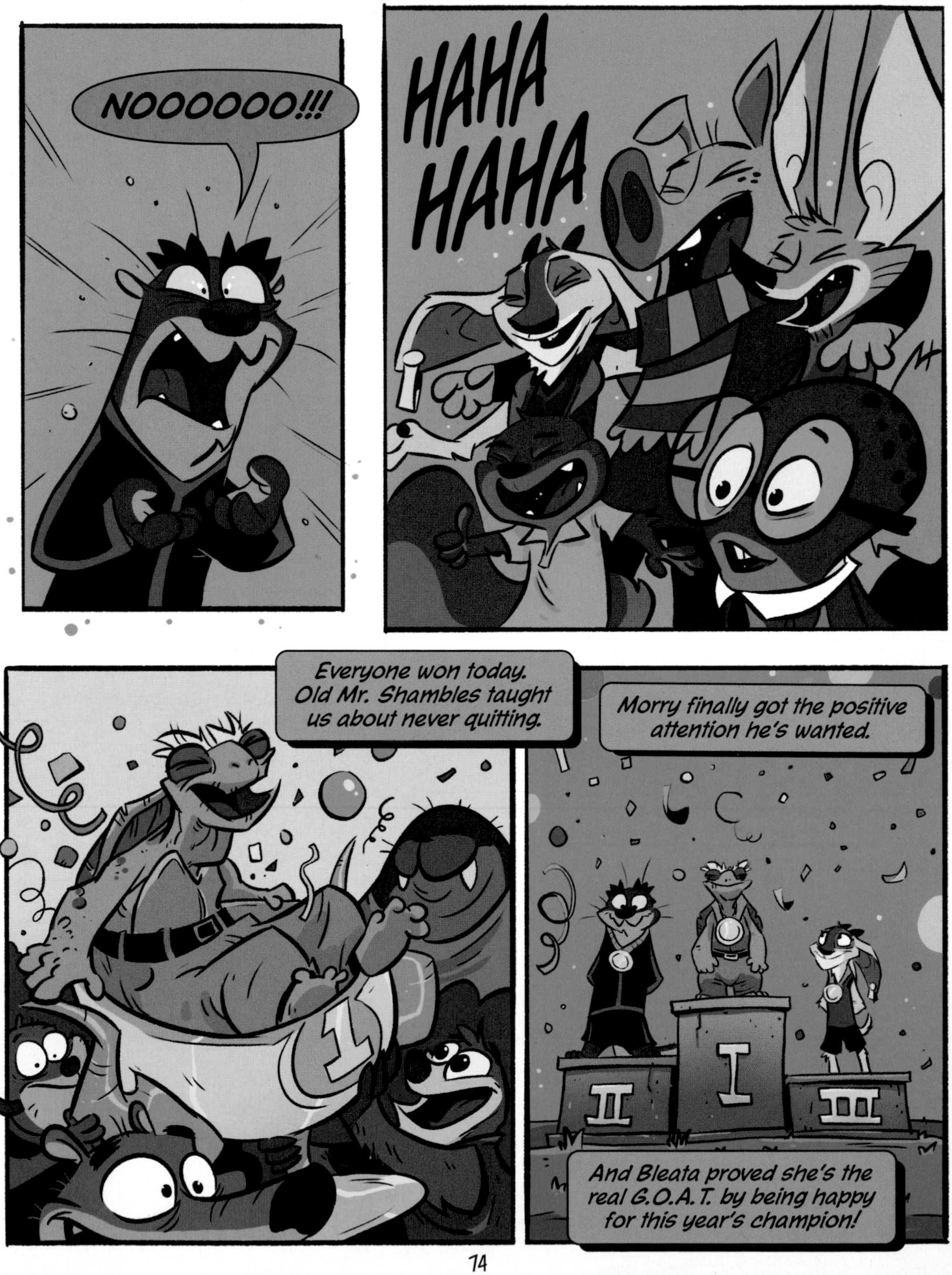
NOOOOOO!!!
HAHA HAHA
Everyone won today. Old Mr. Shambles taught us about never quitting.
Morry finally got the positive attention he's wanted.
I
II
III
And Bleata proved she's the real G.O.A.T. by being happy for this year's champion!

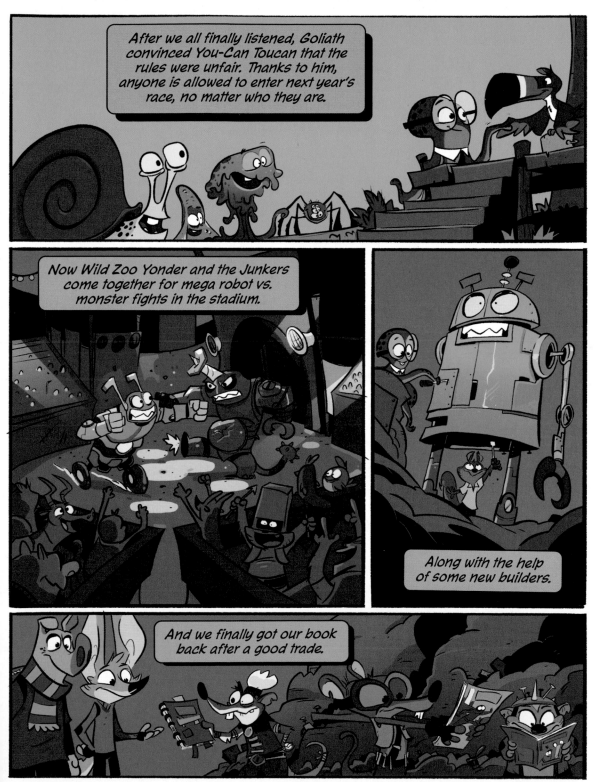

After we all finally listened, Goliath convinced You-Can Toucan that the rules were unfair. Thanks to him, anyone is allowed to enter next year's race, no matter who they are.

Now Wild Zoo Yonder and the Junkers come together for mega robot vs. monster fights in the stadium.

Along with the help of some new builders.

And we finally got our book back after a good trade.

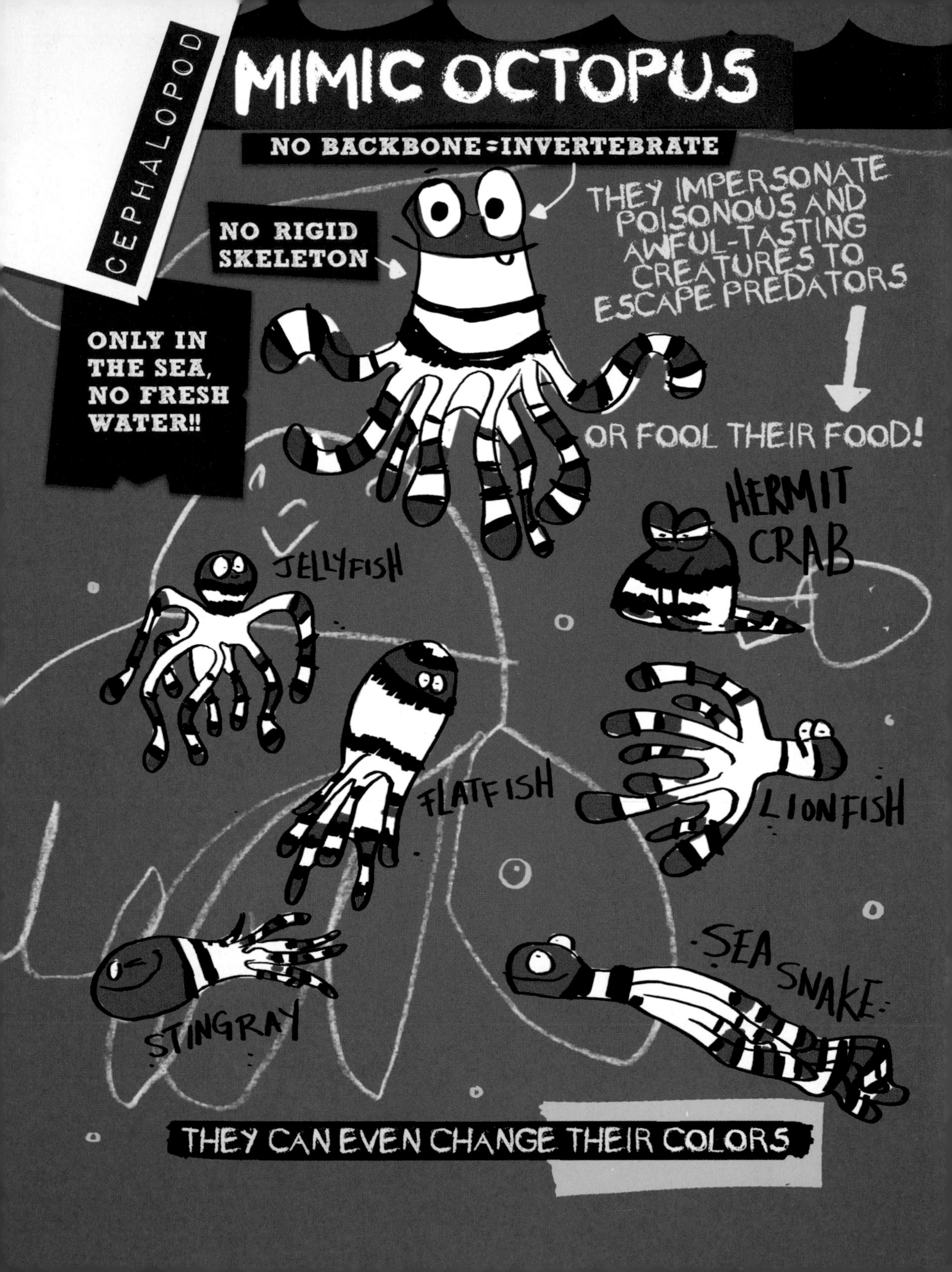
CEPHALOPOD
MIMIC OCTOPUS
NO BACKBONE=INVERTEBRATE
NO RIGID SKELETON
THEY IMPERSONATE POISONOUS AND AWFUL-TASTING CREATURES TO ESCAPE PREDATORS
ONLY IN THE SEA, NO FRESH WATER!!
OR FOOL THEIR FOOD!
HERMIT CRAB
JELLYFISH
FLATFISH
LIONFISH
SEA SNAKE
STINGRAY
THEY CAN EVEN CHANGE THEIR COLORS

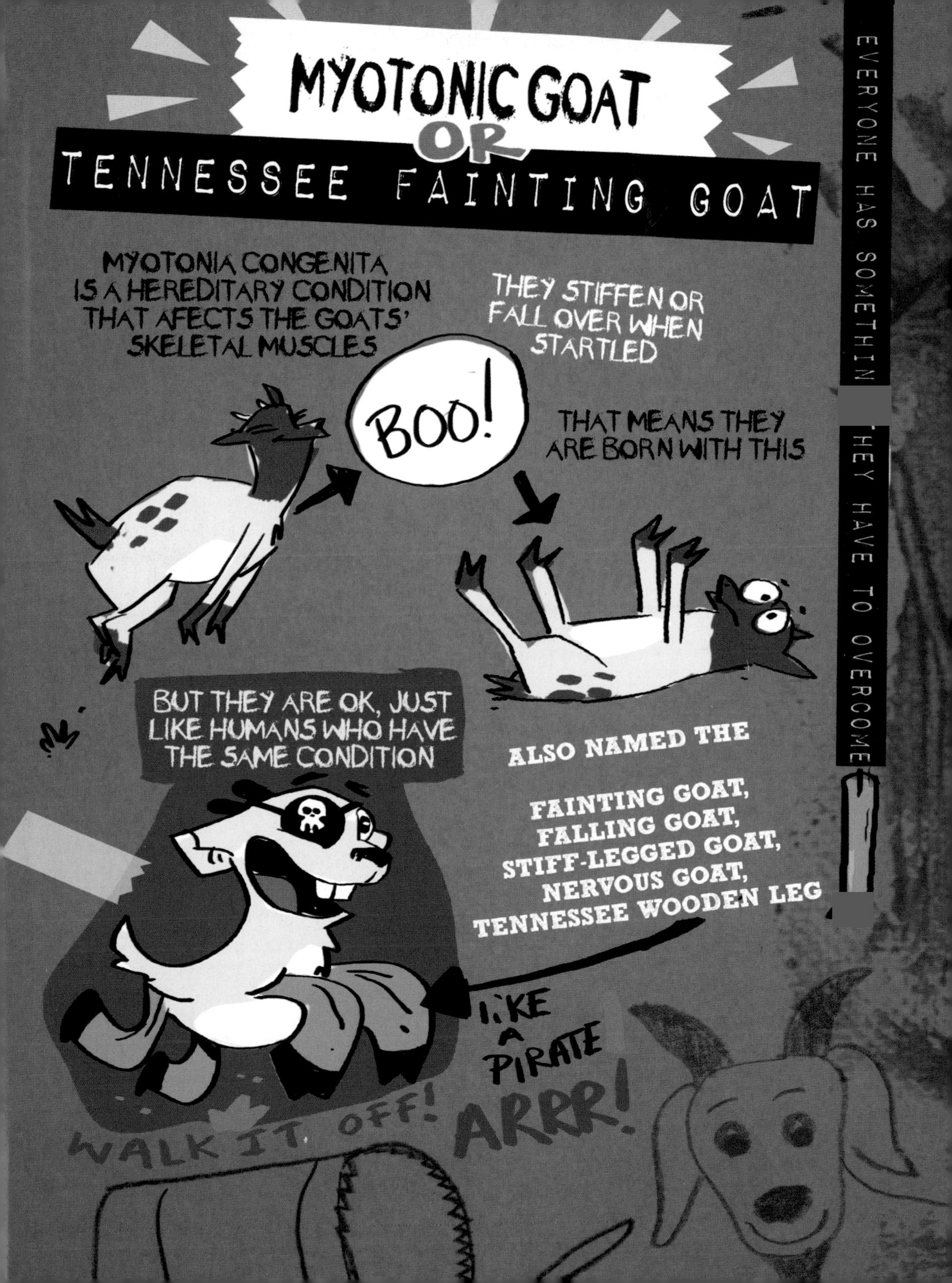

MYOTONIC GOAT
OR
TENNESSEE FAINTING GOAT
MYOTONIA CONGENITA IS A HEREDITARY CONDITION THAT AFECTS THE GOATS' SKELETAL MUSCLES
THEY STIFFEN OR FALL OVER WHEN STARTLED
BOO!
THAT MEANS THEY ARE BORN WITH THIS
BUT THEY ARE OK, JUST LIKE HUMANS WHO HAVE THE SAME CONDITION
ALSO NAMED THE
FAINTING GOAT,
FALLING GOAT,
STIFF-LEGGED GOAT,
NERVOUS GOAT,
TENNESSEE WOODEN LEG
LIKE A PIRATE
ARRR!
WALK IT OFF!
EVERYONE HAS SOMETHIN
HEY HAVE TO OVERCOME

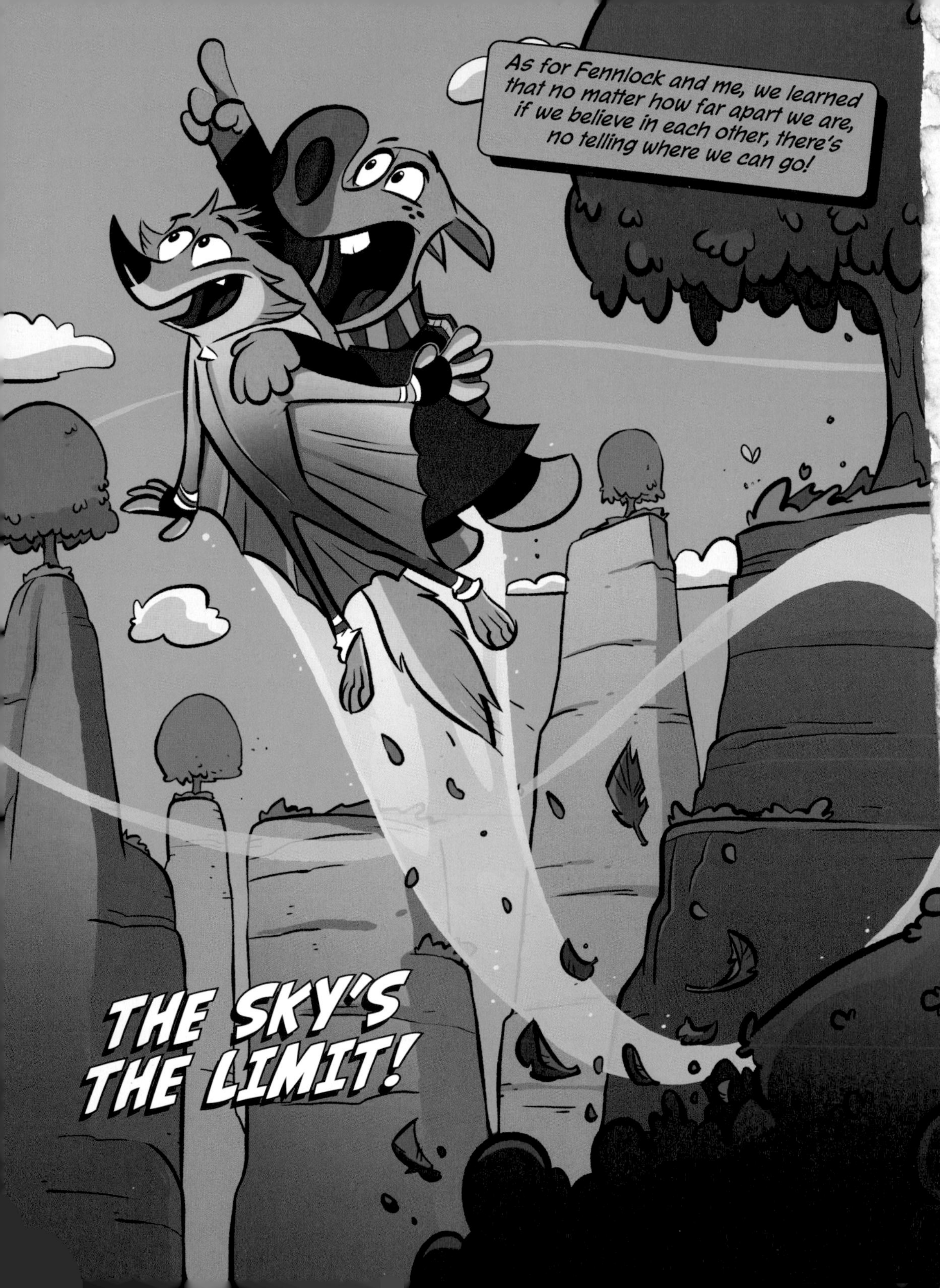
As for Fennlock and me, we learned that no matter how far apart we are, if we believe in each other, there's no telling where we can go!
THE SKY'S THE LIMIT!